REVIEWS

"Tour Secrets kept my undivided attention from beginning to end and it has me eagerly waiting to read the sequel. Tour Secrets is a phenomenal debut by Winkk."

APOOO Bookclub

"The portrayal of the tour and celebrity lifestyle is a must read for those who are oblivious to the discrimination, favoritism, and jealousy. Tour Secrets is definitely a novel that will raise more than a few eyebrows."

Urban Reviews

"This book was a page turner and I couldn't wait to see what was going to happen next. This is a must read."

Worldwide Readers

A NOVEL BY

WINK Katme

Ailam Publishing LLC
P.O. Box 43413
Chicago, IL 60643
www.ailampublishing.com

ISBN 978-0-9837759-1-1
Library of Congress Control Number: 2011912094

First Ailam Publishing LLC trade paperback edition September 2011

Book Cover Concept by: Winkk and Graphix by Dzine
Book Cover Design by: Graphix by Dzine
Book Cover Photography by: Reginald Payton
Book Cover Model/Dancer: Regina Daniels

10 9 8 7 6 5 4 3 2 1

Manufactured in the United States of America

To order additional copies of this book contact:

Ailam Publishing LLC
ailampublishing@aol.com
P.O. Box 43413, Chicago, IL 60643
www.ailampublishing.com

Acknowledgements

I thank God for being by my side and carrying me through this journey. I trust and love the lord and will never stray away from his direction. This has been an amazing and difficult ride. It has always been my dream to write novels and I finally got the courage and strength to do it. I could not have done this without the help of my family and friends. Their encouragement and support carried me through this journey.

I thank my husband, for allowing me to write and follow my dreams. Thanks for listening to my stories every day; all day long and still showing excitement. Thanks for being my second set of eyes. I love you. To my daughter, I love you so much. I also want to thank you for jumping on my head and banging on my computer while I was trying to finish the book. You taught me how to continue to work during many distractions. ☺ There's a lesson in every situation.

To my Mom and dad thank you for telling me "Don't stop! Keep writing." You encouraged me to continue no matter what and I love you dearly for the support. You are my best friends and my support system. Thanks for always being my biggest fan. You have taught me to work hard and get what I want out of life.

To my fabulous sister Marcia thank you for all the fashion tips. Just to know that you were willing to help made me happy. Thanks for being the model for the project. The photo shoot was wonderful and you looked beautiful. Thanks for all your support. Love you. To my handsome and talented brother Alven, you have stepped in and helped me in many ways and I thank you. I appreciate your excitement for the project and always continuing to lend a hand. You know I love you and I always got your back. You're the hottest producer I know and the track on my website and video trailers proves it. To my other fabulous sister Montoya, thank you for the style and confidence you give me daily. I appreciate you letting me read parts of my book to you. I love your advice, opinions and laughter. I really needed your support and you were always there for me. Love you.

I give thanks to Anita for being my right arm and left ear in this process. I thank you for being just as excited as I am and constantly encouraging me to continue. You were a major part in this. Let's do this. To my little sis Ebony Mitchell, I thank you for being the model for this project. Your pictures were fabulous and you are the "Next Super Model". I know we will see more things from you in the future. I can't wait to read your novel. To my sister Tamala, thanks for always supporting me. Thank you for reading the book and giving your suggestions and advice. Also, thanks for helping to put together a wonderful and exciting book release celebration. I appreciate you supporting me.

Regina Daniels, I thank you for gracing the cover of my books with those wonderful legs. It was a pleasure working with you. You are a wonderful person and a great dancer.

Words can't explain how I feel about Sharon King. You gave me the nudge I needed to get this project off the ground. Thank you for the encouragement, advice and critiques. You were the very first person I allowed to read my manuscripts. When I didn't think I could do it, you told me I could. You definitely encouraged me to keep writing and I thank you for that. To my nefrew Phil, you are the coolest person I know at such a young age. I love you and can't wait to support your career. It's time to drop your album.

An Inside Job Production: Thanks for planning an exciting, fun and unique Book Release Celebration. You paid attention to every detail and provided me with a celebration I will remember forever. To Reginald Payton: Thanks for taking great pictures for the cover of my book. I appreciate you being patient with my creative craziness. To Teranz Boutiques: Thanks for the HOT outfit. You have some unique clothes.

No one can touch your fabulous outfits. To Graphix by Dzine: Thanks for listening to my creativity and allowing my imagination to become reality for the book cover and website.

Special thanks to: Self Pro Motion, Poison Ivy dance group, Boys of Poison dance group, Lorenzo, Captain Black, Herman, Prototype, Koolaid, Nicole, Tony Binns, Rolling Out Magazine, Art Sims "Chat Daddy", John Smith, Choklit Jok Morning Jumpoff Show, Power 92 Radio, Merrlyn, Andre Fluker, 102.3FM, Carla Dean, Raw TV, WVON Radio, Terrance Douglas, WCSU, Johariel Hair Salon, Ty Ku Liquors, Remy Martin, Vince Bass, Mary Datcher, Metropolis, APOOO Bookclub, Urban Reviews, LOL Bookclub, Myspace fans, Facebook fans, Twitter fans and Parle Magazine. Thanks to all the readers for holding me down on this project and enjoying the words that poured from my mind.

I also can't stress enough how much my family stepped in and carried me. You guys are my biggest cheerleaders and I'm so grateful. I know I'm forgetting somebody but please forgive me. I have no more brain cells left. I would like to thank everyone for listening to me talk about the book ALL THE TIME. I'm sure I got on your nerves, but you never showed it. Thanks for listening and supporting. Let's continue to motivate, inspire and support each other.

Love ya,

Nikki

TOUR SECRETS

by W I N K Katme

Music and Raven are determined to make it in the music industry as dancers and they immerse themselves into a world of sex, money and betrayal. A secret is revealed that will challenge their friendship and dreams. Faced with drama, lies, abuse and even murder, they manage to penetrate deeper into the music industry as dancers on tour for Slyy, one of the industry's most famous recording artist. Their lives will be devastated forever from his tour.

One issue after another, they realize that trying to accomplish a dream that everyone wants is difficult to acquire and maintain. They soon find out that making it as dancers in the music industry is challenging, but surviving on the road and keeping secrets is almost impossible. Delve behind the scenes into the lives of dancers who bring 'flavor' to the stages around the world to create memorable shows for sold out concerts.

CHAPTER 1

"Please sign in and have your pictures and resume available. We will call your name when we're ready for you," the receptionist said as Raven and I entered the building of the dance audition.

The well-known dance studio was over crowded with beautiful, limber dancers waiting to show their skills for the group, Riff Raff, new music video. Some dancers were trying to find a place to stretch, while others rehearsed and fixed their hair. Most of them had on entirely too much make-up and their clothes were extremely tight.

Raven and I didn't believe in wearing a lot of make-up to auditions, and felt that look should be saved for the stage. We were beautiful with or without make-up, and we wore just enough to accent our beauty and play up our natural look.

Being 5'5" with dark skin, high cheekbones, an hour glass figure, long hair and grey eyes, which were all natural, gave me a look ready for stardom. People described me as a combination of Chili from the group TLC, because of my hair, and the model Naomi Campbell, because of my bone structure, complexion and full lips.

I've always received weird comments from strangers about my complexion. "You're beautiful to be dark-skinned," was a remark I heard on a regular basis. I didn't know if it was a compliment or an insult.

Society made people think light-skinned girls were gorgeous and if you were dark-skinned, you were not attractive. I didn't believe that theory at all. I loved and embraced the color of my skin. I was chocolate, beautiful and confident.

In the entertainment industry, dark-skinned people didn't get any respect and they made it much harder for us to succeed, especially if you were a woman. Racism was something I despised, but was forced to get accustomed to. Although I was determined to be a dancer, I struggled during the process.

Raven was the complete package, standing 5'9 with four inch stilettos on. She had a striking shapely body, large breast, a small waist with an undeniable gorgeous face. She was a light-skin lively Latino, with a beautiful smile, exotic eyes, and a short sexy hairstyle, reminding you of the singer Rihanna.

Because Raven was Latino, she didn't have to deal with the type of discrimination I dealt with. However, she always defended me when someone was disrespectful because of my complexion.

Raven and I found a spot in the corner of the studio and prepared to dance. Looking around, we noticed a lot of the same dancers we see at every audition. We were a little nervous, but ready to show them what we had.

"What school did you train at?" A dancer asked us.

"We didn't train at a school," I told her.

"You must be some of those self-taught dancers," she said very snooty-like, then turned around and started whispering to her friends.

"Yes, we're self-taught. Is that a problem?" Raven asked with a snappy attitude.

"This audition is for real dancers. I hope you can hang," she replied with a smirk.

"I just hope you can keep up," I said, staring her down.

"It won't be hard keeping up with you," the dancer said as she kicked her leg high.

Stooping to her level, I kicked my leg higher and frowned at her. I wasn't about to let her think she could out do me. This was the childish behavior dancers had, and I couldn't help but be involved with it.

"Why are you talking to us?" Raven said as she stepped closer to the dancer.

"I can talk to whoever I want to," the dancer said.

"Look bitch, you don't want me to mop this floor with your ass," Raven said.

"Don't let my beauty fool you. I will beat the hell out of you," the dancer said, not backing down.

"Now you know that's not going to happen. So, step off before I show you whose ass is going to get beat," I said clenching my teeth, as I walked closer to her.

"What are you going to do? You uppity bitch," the dancer said.

Before I could say another word, Raven quickly smacked her face. The girl looked stunned and thought about the scene we were making. She was more interested in getting the job, then getting kicked out of the audition for fighting. She didn't expect Raven to hit her and wasn't prepared to get into a battle.

I grabbed Raven's arm and we quickly walked away from the scene. Since it was so crowded, the altercation wasn't seen by the people holding the auditions, and only a few dancers had witnessed it. Sadly, we were used to getting into arguments with other dancers. It was something we had become familiar with.

If you were not a trained dancer, you were not respected. Dancing was in our blood, so, trained or not, we were confident with our skills, and didn't want to constantly be harassed about it. We knew once we started dancing, no one would be concerned about where we went to school, and would see unquestionable excellent dance skills.

The difference between us and other dancers, is dancing is their only source of income. Raven and I have full-time jobs and we are not depending on dancing at this moment to make a living. So, if we didn't get the job, we didn't get too depressed because our bills were not getting paid. Instead, we worked harder and waited for the next audition.

Strangely, I felt guilty getting paid for something I loved doing because most people didn't have the opportunity to experience it. I would love to quit my regular job and dance full time, and I'm hoping that going to these auditions would help me accomplish that soon.

When the auditions started, I began to get anxious. I didn't like the whole process, and I hated competing against other dancers, but knew I had to get used to it in order to succeed in this business. On the other hand, Raven was ready and thrived off of the competition.

Looking at all the beautiful dancers made me a little intimidated. Dancers were cut throat and ruthless, and we had to learn how to handle them. Dealing with unnecessary drama, was one part of the business that we detested.

"Music, you're next," the receptionist announced.

Raven wished me luck and waited for her name to be called.

I walked into the room with ten people inside watching me quietly. I could dance in front of thousands of people, but dancing in front of a small crowd, made me extremely uneasy. I shook off my nervousness, handed a man at the door my music, and told him to play track number two. I planned on combining several types of dances into my routine, including African, jazz, and hip-hop.

After the music started, I felt the beat and immediately started moving. I started off doing a triple turn and then went right into some sexy reggae moves to show them that I was versatile. When I did the triple turn, the judges started clapping.

I started dancing sexy and their mouths fell to the floor. I finished with a few hip-hop and ballet moves. By the look on their faces, I felt like they were impressed. I had a great performance and was optimistic about being hired.

Once I was done, I told Raven what to expect. Her audition went great, as well, and she also showed her versatility with her dance moves. She said they were captivated by her audition.

Once all the dancers had auditioned, the judges made us get into two groups they assembled, and made us stand while they looked us up and down like we were pieces of meat. They even asked some of the dancers to turn around so they could get a good view of their bodies.

We felt so cheap, but we wanted the job. Raven's group was told to sit down, and to my surprise, my group was told to go home. They thanked us for coming and sent us out of the room and building immediately.

They hired six light-skinned girls, and I was disappointment I was not one of them, but happy Raven had gotten the job. I hated going to auditions knowing it was going to be a fight to get hired because of my dark complexion.

It was obvious I didn't fit into their color scheme. Raven and I were used to the color criteria and supported each other no matter what. As long as one of us was hired, we were happy.

A few days later, I got a call from the casting director of the Riff Raff audition. One of the dancers got sick and was unable to do the video the next day, so they offered me the job.

I wanted to tell them to go to hell since the only reason they were calling me was because they were in a jam, but I knew better than to turn down the job. I was excited but offended at the same time.

All the dancers had a week to prepare for the music video and listen to the group's new song, and I had less than eight hours. I had to always be prepared to survive these last minutes jobs.

The casting director told me the dancers were going to freestyle and they would not be providing clothes. I had to be on set the next day at four o'clock in the morning, and I wasn't happy about the early call-time. I didn't hesitate to call Raven and she was ecstatic about us working together.

Raven and I walked on set of the Riff Raff music video at three thirty in the morning and immediately felt like it was going to be a long, uncomfortable day. This was definitely a low-budget video, and it was being filmed at an old abandoned dirty warehouse, giving them an industrial look which was the concept for the video.

All the dancers were squeezed into a small hot room, and we tried to find a place to start doing our make-up, since they didn't provide a make-up artist for us. Raven and I were starving and happy they had donuts and coffee for everyone.

They had been shooting the video for about four hours and Raven and some of the other dancers were still working, while I was waiting for them to call me. I didn't know any of the girls, and once again, I was the token dark-skinned dancer.

Finally they were ready to start shooting more dancers and started calling us one by one. Unfortunately, they didn't call my name again, and I continued waiting. By now, I was the only dancer they had not chosen, and some of the other dancers were selected twice for different scenes. It was embarrassing, but I tried to act like it didn't bother me.

"We're taking a thirty-minute break for dinner. Enjoy the pizza," one of the crew members told everyone. Then he turned to one of the dancers and said, "We're going to shoot you again after dinner, so be ready."

By now, I was frustrated and wanted to know when I was going to shoot because it seemed like they didn't even notice me. Raven was upset, but knew how the business was and she knew not to say anything about it.

At dinner, we overheard the crew talking about how they loved Raven and a few of the other dancers they had filmed so far. Raven and I continued eavesdropping as the assistant director started talking to the crew.

"What was up with those last dancers?" A crew member asked.

"They were horrible. Only a few of the dancers are giving them what they want," The assistant director said as he stuffed pizza in his mouth.

"They haven't filmed the dark-skinned dancer. Why are they not using her?" The crew member asked the assistant director.

"Man, you know Riff Raff isn't into dark meat," the assistant director responded.

"She's sexy. Why did they hire her if they were not going to use her?"

"I don't know. That's just how the business is. They like what they like. She'll get paid, though."

Knowing that they discriminated was one thing, but hearing it hurt me deeply. You have to develop thick skin in this business to make it. Raven knew it really bothered me, but also knew I would get over it. She was sad but knew she had to do what she was hired to do, which was dance.

It was nine o'clock at night and I was still waiting. I'm aware that in this business you have to hurry up and wait, but this was ridiculous. Finally, a crew member came into the room and looked around at the dancers. They had picked some of the dancers twice and had not picked me even once. The crew member felt badly because he knew he was purposely overlooking me, but he was just following instructions.

He stared at me and said, "Are you ready to work?"

"Yes, I've been ready," I replied.

Once I got on set, everyone turned around and looked at me strangely. I'm not sure if they were looking at me because I was not supposed to be there, or if they thought I would not deliver like the rest of the girls. When Raven saw me, she smiled and knew I was about to let them have it.

Sounding as though he was tired and irritated, the director gave me some brief instructions.

"Dance around the group and be sexy. Can you be sexy?" He asked me in a nasty tone.

"Yes," I told him.

The music started and it was show time. I danced around the group like a professional, dancing sexy and working some great moves in. While I danced, they turned on a fan and my hair started blowing.

The director told Raven to join me on the set, and we completely went out of control. They were so impressed, that they let us keep dancing for the entire song.

The problem with the other dancers was that they were looking too sluttish and the director wanted sex appeal. By the time we finished, the director was clapping.

"That's what I'm looking for. We should have used you sooner. Putting Raven with you was the icing on the cake. You both are beautiful. We could have been done shooting a long time ago," the director said pleased.

The group was happy with my performance and used me for other shots. It's a shame they didn't want to use me because of the color of my skin.

When the video was shown on television, Raven and I were the only dancers they showed. All the other dancers were used as extras. I was shocked to see they gave me several close up shots.

Afterwards, my telephone didn't stop ringing for dance jobs. I felt like I had represented and opened the doors for dark-skinned women. We were now considered sexy and beautiful in the music industry.

CHAPTER 2

"Turn the radio up. That's my song," Raven said, while dancing around her bedroom.

"If you stop singing so loud, you could hear it," I told her, as I started putting on my clothes.

We were getting ready to perform at a show and were in the middle of our normal ritual, which was playing music, dancing and getting dressed. We always had a great time preparing for our shows, which hyped us up and got our adrenaline pumping.

"I'm going to take a quick shower, so turn the music up," Raven said, as she put her shower cap on and got in the tub.

"How loud do you want me to blast it? Just wait until you get out," I shouted, while continuing to get dress.

Raven continued to sing while she took a shower, so I gave in and blasted our favorite song on the radio to drown her out.

Like an old married couple, we always argued, but this was how we communicated. The arguments were never anything too serious, just heated debates that usually turned into friendly conversations.

Raven and I had been friends since childhood, and we both had a common interest, which was dancing. Our love of dance is what started our friendship and continued to fuel it. Our dream was to dance on tour, travel the world with platinum-selling recording artists, meet exciting people, and make lots of money. We were working very hard to turn our dreams into reality.

When I first met Raven, she was an outcast and didn't hang around many people. Being the outgoing and popular one at the time, I always tried to get her to break out of her shell.

She was a great dancer and I wanted her to be a part of my dance group. Finally, after bugging her every day, she decided to start dancing with us, and we were happy she did. Raven fit with us perfectly, which helped her to become more comfortable with herself.

Our group had a few dancers who were trained and some were still attending dance school. The rest of us were self-taught, and we learned how to dance from watching videos and practicing daily. We were just as skilled as the trained dancers were, and very comfortable working together because we complemented each other well on stage.

Our specialties were jazz, ballet, hip-hop, African and contemporary dance. We were very versatile and each had our own style. We had paid our dues and were on the right path to making it as successful dancers in the music industry.

After dancing together for such a long time, some of the dancers in the group wanted to perform solo and others had their own agendas. Although we supported everyone's decision, Raven and I were not ready to dance solo, so, we decided to start a new adventure by dancing together.

We were like Batman and Robin. Raven was Latino, with beautiful skin that looked like white chocolate, and I was African American, with beautiful dark-chocolate skin that was bronzed by the sun. We both had an exotic look and considered ourselves the dynamic duo of dancing.

I choreographed the routines, while Raven made the moves look smooth and hot. We were both offering beauty and talent. We had the full package and were ready to take over the world. Although we missed dancing with our group, we knew we could still continue without them.

Like the typical dancer, Raven was happy at the moment being in the background, but dreamed of eventually being in the main spotlight. Once you've followed someone for so long, you wanted to be the leader. I had no worries, because I knew Raven wouldn't get caught up in the music industry that she would change.

We always gave each other reality checks to keep us grounded. She was my best friend. I trusted her, she trusted me, and no amount of fame or fortune would ever change that.

Raven was my personal beauty consultant and taught me how to put on make-up, as well as how to act like a lady. She introduced me to the finer things in life, such as Prada, Gucci, Christian Louboutin, Manolo Blahnik, and other designer labels.

She taught me how to work what I had to get what I wanted. She was truly skilled at getting whatever she needed without working hard for it. Raven always told me that women didn't know their power, and the power we had was between our legs.

I loved Raven like a sister, even though we were very different. She was light-skinned; I was dark-skinned. She was the bad girl; I was the good girl. We were complete opposites, but it seemed to work just fine for our friendship.

While Raven sung loudly in the shower, her cell phone started ringing. I was so wrapped up in my dancing that I decided not to let her know she had a call, and to let it go to voicemail. Someone was really trying to contact her, I thought, because her phone kept ringing.

Reluctantly, I yelled for Raven to tell her that her phone was ringing, but she didn't answer. So, I slightly opened the bathroom door just enough to stick my head in, while holding her cell phone in my hand.

"Raven, don't you hear me calling you? Your cell phone is ringing off the hook," I shouted, opening the bathroom door wider as the steam from the shower hit me in my face.

Because of the music blasting, the shower running, and her loud off-key singing, Raven didn't hear me. She was shocked when she stepped out of the shower and saw me standing in the doorway.

I dropped her cell phone and stood frozen. I rubbed my eyes, blinked a couple of times, and then opened them extremely wide to see clearly.

"Music, get out of here!" Raven yelled, as she hopped back into the tub and closed the shower curtain quickly.

"What the hell is that?" I asked confused.

"Get out!" She yelled again very sternly.

Raven would not come from behind the shower curtain, and I continued standing there, refusing to leave.

"I'm not going anywhere. Get your ass out of the shower," I demanded.

After a few seconds of silence and realizing she wasn't going to come out on her own, I rushed to the bathtub and yanked the shower curtain so hard that it came off the hooks and fell to the floor.

Raven was standing in the tub with a towel wrapped around her, which I quickly snatched off. She tried to stop me, but I was too fast. She stood in the tub naked, never moving.

I looked at her flat chest that used to have large breast. Then, I glanced down at where her vagina should have been, but miraculously it had vanished. I was totally flabbergasted. Raven just looked at me without saying a word.

"You have a dick! Are you going to say something?" I snapped, while grabbing her exposed genitals. "Is this thing real?"

Raven ran out of the bathroom and into her bedroom with me right behind her. As she grabbed a robe to put on, I quickly pushed her down on the floor.

"You better say something!" I yelled.

"Get off of me," she said sadly, as she started crying.

Her tears didn't faze me. I didn't know how I was feeling, but baffled would be an accurate description. Raven lied to me, betrayed my trust, and she now felt like a stranger.

“I’m getting out of here,” I told her, as I started getting my things.

“Don’t leave, Music. Let me talk to you,” she pleaded.

“No, you’re a freak and I’m leaving now!” I yelled.

After hearing all the commotion coming from Raven’s bedroom, her mother stuck her head in the door. “What’s going on?”

“Raven has a dick!” I blurted out to her mother, as a gloomy look came over her face.

Her mother stepped inside and closed the door slowly.

“Music, please sit down so we can talk,” Raven’s mother said, as she looked at Raven and asked, “Why didn’t you tell her?”

“Tell me what? That she has a penis. I can see that,” I replied very angrily. When no one said a word, I continued. “Raven, why did you lie to me? You should have told me the truth.” Then, I immediately started laughing uncontrollably. “Is this some kind of joke?

Raven was crying and rocking herself in the corner of the bedroom, never saying a word.

“Music, please sit down and hear me out,” her mother said, as she began telling their family secret.

Raven was born a boy and her real name was Randy. As a baby, everyone mistook Raven for a girl. Her mother wanted a girl so desperately she dressed Raven in pretty ruffle dresses and put pink ribbons in her hair. She deliberately manipulated people into believing she was a girl. She never let anyone get close enough to her to reveal Raven’s secret. She even changed her name on her birth certificate to make her officially Raven.

“Unbelievable,” I said still shocked.

“I feel responsible for all of this,” Raven’s mother said.

“You’re not responsible, Mom. I’m a woman now and I’ll never be a man,” Raven screamed from the corner of the bedroom.

Tears ran down her mother’s face as she struggled to continue speaking. “When Raven got older, I had a talk with her and told her that she was not a girl, but indeed a boy. I asked her if she wanted to live her life as a boy or a girl. I wanted it to be her decision."

I quickly interrupted her. "You had already made that choice for her."

"You're right, and I have to live everyday with that guilt," her mother said.

Raven felt like a girl on the inside, and therefore wanted to look like one on the outside. Her mother promised to never tell anyone and that she would pay for her to have a sex change when she got older.

Her mother left the room and returned with a box full of pictures of Raven. I looked at them in disbelief because she didn't look like a boy in the pictures.

"Raven, you could have told me the truth. We're best friends and tell each other everything," I said, while observing her.

"I was afraid you would judge me. I wanted you to like me," Raven admitted sadly.

I looked at Raven, who was still crying and rocking in the corner, and then at her baby pictures. Her mother's tears never stopped running down her face. I didn't know if they were both crazy or just made a terrible mistake. I loved Raven like a sister, and up until now, she had never done anything to hurt me.

"Raven is finally feeling comfortable in her own skin and people really like her. Ever since she started dancing with you, she has become a different person. Dancing made her more confident. Please don't make her go back into that shell she was once in," her mother said, as she grabbed my hand and begged for me to maintain their secrecy.

With all the craziness going on, we forgot we had to perform at a show in less than an hour. I wanted to cancel and go home to deal with this situation, but I knew we couldn't. Instead, we finished getting dressed and left for the show without saying another word to each other.

We made it through the show like professionals, but it was not our normal performance. Our usual connection on stage was no longer there, and immediately after the show, I left without saying a word to her.

On the way home, I kept wondering what people would think if they knew Raven was really a man. I wondered how differently people would treat her if this information got out. I didn't know if people in the music industry would want to hire a transsexual, or if they even cared.

The next day, Raven was ringing my telephone off the hook, but I wasn't ready to talk. I was still perplexed by the whole situation. I repeatedly went over in my head anything that would have given me a clue that she was a man, but I couldn't think of one thing.

We always changed our clothes in front of each other before shows and I never saw anything strange, I guess I wasn't looking for it, either. Raven was well put together and wore a matching bra and panty set just like I did, filling her 34C bra to capacity.

She must have taped her penis down to hide it, because I never saw a bulge in her panties or pants. She always went to the women's bathroom, so there was nothing out of the ordinary that would have made me think she was a man.

It was too much for me to handle. I needed time and a break from Raven, Randy, or whoever she was. Over the next several weeks, Raven continued to call me, but I refused to answer. I didn't know if I wanted to continue our friendship, because I didn't know what else she was lying about.

~~~~~~~

Unable to keep Raven's secret to myself, I decided to talk to my mother. As I was telling her about Raven, she instantly looked shocked, but immediately changed her expression back to normal.

"Music, what difference does it make what genital parts Raven has? The two of you have been friends since you were kids, and that should not change."

This situation didn't seem too bizarre to her, and I didn't understand why she was so calm about it.
~~~~~~~

"Did you know Raven was a boy?" I asked.

"No, baby, I'm just as shocked as you are," she replied.

"This is a mess," I said.

"This has to be hard for Raven. She's probably hurt and needs you as a friend now more than ever. Never break the trust you have with each other. Secrets are sacred, and you must be able to keep them," she said.

"I've already broken the trust by telling you," I said, disappointed with myself.

"You did the right thing by telling me. I'm your mother. But, don't lose Raven as your friend. I know you're hurt and confused, but those feelings will pass. You have to talk to her and let her express how she's feeling. This will help you understand why she never told you," she replied with deep concern.

"I've been dancing with a man," I said, still dazed.

"And you should continue dancing with her, whether she's a man or a woman. Besides, you won't dance forever. This is just a hobby."

"It's not a hobby; it's my dream," I said, upset with my mother's response.

"We're not going to get into this discussion about your dreams. Just keep dancing with Raven," my mother said happy to avoid talking about my career choice.

"Why are you so calm about this?" I asked.

"Nothing shocks me in today's world," she said, shaking her head.

"Mom, was I really born a girl?" I asked jokingly.

We looked at each other and laughed.

"Thank God you never had to go through that. You're my precious, naturally-born little girl, who is now a woman," she said, then smiled and gave me a kiss on the cheek.

"I love you, Mom," I told her before hugging her tightly.

"I love you, too, baby. Now make sure you talk to Raven. Give her a chance to tell you her side of the story. Don't lose this friendship over something like this."

I covered my face with my hands and took a deep breath.

She smiled and said, "Who else will be your dance partner? You've had enough time to think about it. Now, deal with it."

~~~~~~~

The next day, I called Raven and she picked up on the first ring.

"Raven, we need to talk. Can you stop by my place today?" I asked.

"I'll be there in twenty minutes," she quickly replied.

Next, I called my mother to tell her that Raven was coming to my apartment to talk. I needed some support.

"Mom, I need you here. I can't talk to Raven alone," I said.

"This is something you need to do on your own. Just make her feel as comfortable as possible, and don't look at this like she tried to trick you. Remember, she's in pain and really needs a friend," my mother said before hanging up.

Twenty minutes later, Raven was ringing my doorbell. As I sat listening to her, I could see the sadness and pain in her eyes.

"Music, please forgive me. I never wanted to deceive you, but I didn't know if you could handle the truth. It's hard living in a man's body when you feel like a woman," she confessed, as tears rolled down her face.

"Do you like women or men?" I asked.

"I love men. The only thing a woman can do for me is tell me where she bought her shoes. I love being around women because you guys help me keep my look flawless. Don't worry, sweetie. I don't like you that way," she said sarcastically.

"I didn't think you did, but I wanted to make sure," I replied.
~~~~~~~

"Please don't stop dancing with me. I really want to dance and not be judged because I'm a man doing women dance moves, even though I dance better than any woman I know," Raven said with a smile.

"Boy, you don't dance better than me," I jokingly responded.

We both started laughing, which took the tension away from the conversation.

"I'm not a boy. I'm a grown man under all this fabulousness," Raven said.

"You're now a man and not a boy?" I asked, teasing her.

"Yes, I'm a man, and this large dick that's constantly in the way tells me that every day," Raven said, still laughing.

"We will always dance together. Who else will do my choreography the way you do?" I reassured her.

"No one can do it better than me," she said, while rolling her eyes at me.

"It's going to take me some time to deal with this situation, but your secret is safe with me," I told her as we hugged.

"Thanks, Music. I love you," Raven said.

I quickly pulled away from her and frowned. "You love me? I knew you wanted me."

"Bitch, please! Don't get it twisted. You're not my type."

We laughed and then hugged once more.

"Raven, you really fooled me," I said.

"I work hard at looking like a woman."

"Where do you hide your penis when you put on fitted clothing?" I asked, curious.

She laughed. "Music, only you would get right to the point."

"You have kept this secret from me for years, so now I need to know every little detail," I said seriously.

She then started sharing every personal detail about herself.

"In today's world, it's easy for me to look like a woman. I buy fake breasts and a fake butt to help create my look. It also helps that I have small hands and feet and a small waist," she said.

I stared at Raven intriguingly from head to toe.

"Why are you looking at me like that?" she asked.

"I'm just amazed at how much you really look like a woman," I replied.

"I've studied a long time on how to be a woman, and I don't have room for mistakes."

"I don't think you have to worry about your secret getting out. I'm your best friend, and you fooled me for years."

"Music, I could teach you a couple of things," Raven said.

"What are you going to teach me?" I responded sassily.

"Honey, don't get me started on you," Raven said rather seriously.

I looked at her and rolled my eyes; she smiled. Raven knew she could trust me with her secret and that made our friendship much stronger. She had taught me how to look like a woman. Imagine that.

I found myself staring at her because I would have never thought she was a man. This made me nervous because now I knew I could be fooled by people and never truly know who they are.

Raven looked better than any woman I knew. No one ever suspected that she was actually a "he", and her secret would always be safe with me.

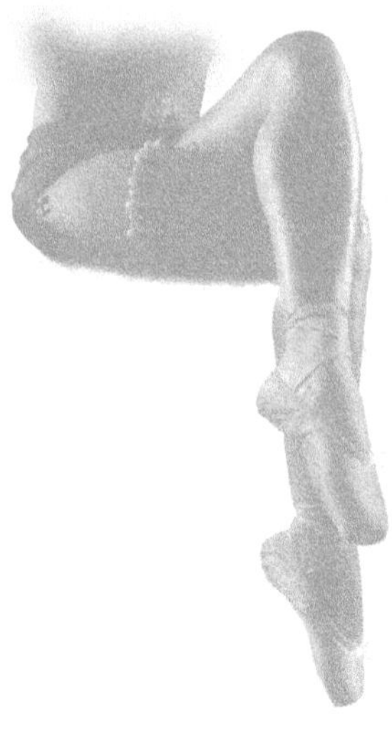

Chapter 3

A few weeks passed, and somehow, I was still upset that Raven didn't tell me exactly who she was. She had lied to me all these years, and I was having a difficult time forgiving and accepting the new Raven.

I thought about how hard it was for her, but I also thought how hard it would be for me to keep it hush-hush. I then started thinking about my father and wondering what he would say about Raven's situation. I knew he would have great advice on how to handle it. He always knew how to make me feel better whenever I was struggling.

"What's up, Music?" Raven asked cheerfully as soon as I answered the telephone.

"Hey Raven. I was just sitting here thinking about my dad."

"I'm surprise you haven't talked about him lately," she said.

"After all this time, it still hurts," I replied softly.

"Are you okay?"

"Yeah, I'll be fine. You know how I have my moments."

"We can talk about it, if you want. It's not good to hold things in."

"I really miss him. Every day I wish he was here with me."

Raven remembered the story about my father, and it will always be fresh in my mind.

My mother became pregnant with me when she was sixteen years old, and her parents were so disappointed that they made her and my father get married. Having a baby and being married at such a young age, people thought they were doomed for disaster. Gratefully, they were in love and made their marriage work.

My mother always told me that getting pregnant and being married was the best thing that ever happened to her. She said she was a wild teenager and that having me made her calm down. She thanked me constantly for being in her life, and continuously told me how she didn't want me to follow in her footsteps.

I started dancing when I was four years old and always enjoyed it. My mother did everything she could to discourage me from dancing. My father, on the other hand, was my best friend and biggest fan. He supported me and really wanted me to follow my dreams. He was always in the front row of every show cheering me on. My dance skills amazed him, and he knew I was capable of being successful.

He told me to never let anyone stop me from following my dreams. Disappointed that he couldn't afford to send me to dance school, he purchased dance videos that I studied every day. He didn't want me to lose focus just because I couldn't get the proper training, so he encouraged me to find other ways to learn.

I taught myself ballet, jazz, contemporary, and hip-hop from watching video tapes and music videos. My dad even bought some used ballet shoes for me to practice in. People were amazed that I could stand up on the Pointe shoes and were even more amazed by the type of dance I did in them.

I could also sing, but I was never interested in it. So, I focused all my attention on dancing. My father enjoyed when I sang and danced for him around the house. He told me that I would be a big star one day. He never could figure out where I got my voice and dance skills from, because neither of my parents had any talent or were even interested in being in the entertainment business.

He said I was blessed and he was going to help me become rich and famous. He always told me to stand up for what I believed in and to never let people walk over me. My strength and toughness came from my father, and my kind heart and drive came from my mother.

We were a normal happy family, until one day our lives changed. It was my tenth birthday, and I was waiting for my father to come home. He had a surprise for me and was going to take me out somewhere special. I waited and waited, but he never showed up. Getting worried, my mother kept calling him, but got no answer. Hours had past and we were still waiting. I wasn't worried, though, because I knew my father would come home soon.

There was a knock on the door, and my mother opened it quickly.

"Hello, Mrs. Jameson, can I come in?" The police officer asked.

My mother immediately started crying when she saw my father's partner.

"What's wrong, Mom?" I asked, as she kept crying.

The police officer walked into our home and three other officers followed behind him.

"Where's my dad?" I asked.

"Please sit down," the officer told me.

When I looked at my mother crying and saw the sad look on the officer's face, I began to cry, as well.

"Where's my daddy?" I asked over and over again.

It was obvious my mother already knew that answer. My father had worked with the police department for four years, and one thing my mother knew was when your husband doesn't come home and his partner shows up at your door, there is something seriously wrong.

"Mrs. Jameson, I'm so sorry to inform you that your husband was shot and killed today," the one officer said, as he took my mother's hand in his.

My father's partner couldn't say a word. He just sat in the chair quietly.

"Oh God!" My mother hollered, like someone had stabbed her.

I couldn't believe it. I kept screaming, "I want my daddy!"

The officers tried to console us, but there was nothing they could do to help. Even though, tears were flowing and my mother's heart was broken into little pieces, she wanted to know what happened to her husband. The officer reluctantly gave her all the details.

My father was shot and killed by a driver when he pulled him over for a traffic violation. The driver had only been out of prison for a week and had just robbed a gas station five minutes before my father noticed him speeding.

Unaware of the crime that was just committed, my father walked up to the car window to ask the driver for his license and registration. The driver didn't want to go back to jail, so before my father could start talking, he was shot in the head as soon he bent down to the driver's window.

Our ears were bleeding and I felt numb inside. I couldn't believe someone would hurt my father. He was such a loving and caring man. Who would want to hurt him? I couldn't accept that I would never see him again.

"We will take you to the hospital to identify the body," the officer said, as they escorted us out of the house.

It seemed like we would never recover from the death of my father. My mother struggled to keep moving, and I stayed with my auntie until my mother was able to function. I became depressed and didn't want to live, but my auntie fought to keep me from going completely crazy. She made me continue dancing, which kept my mind off of the pain.

I started to feel like I was close to my father whenever I danced because I knew he wanted me to succeed. So, using the memory of my father, I dove completely into my dancing career.

A year after his death, my mother decided to move us to Chicago. Living in California constantly reminded her of my father and she wanted to move on with her life. She was tired of being depressed. She desperately wanted the pain to go away, but it seemed like it never would.

I didn't want to leave, but I couldn't take it either. I was hoping Chicago would mend our hearts and help us to move on with our lives. My auntie and cousin Sydney decided to move with us to help with the transition.

We moved to Chicago in a house next door to Raven. She and I quickly became friends since we both were new to the neighborhood. I didn't talk much when I arrived, but Raven seemed to understand and didn't pressure me to relive my nightmare.

Raven was born in Chicago and knew the area well, so she became my personal tour guide. We quickly became best friends and I felt comfortable talking to her. We had a connection that continued to grow.

My cousin Sydney was a few years older than me, and I didn't hang around her much, but she was always there for me. She took the roll of my older sister since I was an only child.

When I got older and my mother realized dancing was not just a phase for me, but that I was serious about it, she spent all her time trying to convince me to do something else. She wanted me to go to college to become a lawyer, and she didn't even want to hear me talking about dancing. It was a struggle for me, but Raven was right by my side. I was upset with my mom for not supporting me like Raven's mother supported her dance career.

I tried to make my mother happy by enrolling in college, but since I was still dancing, she was still disappointed. The more shows I was hired to do, the more she became furious. She didn't want me to be in the music industry and was very distraught that I kept moving forward with my dance career.

Frustrated that she would not support me, this made us argue all the time. So, when I turned eighteen, I got a job and moved out of her house. Having my own apartment made my mother and me happy, and we were then able to talk without arguing.

"Music, are you still there?" Raven asked.

"I'm here. Sorry," I said.

"I got your back and I'm here for you."

"Thanks Raven."

"I know you miss your father, but at least you got a chance to get to know him and have a real family. I don't know who my father is."

"I'm sorry, Raven. I forgot."

"It's cool. I never met him, so I can't miss him."

"I guess."

"Keep living and reach your dreams. I know your mother is still not supportive of your dance career, but you don't need her."

"She doesn't support me," I replied angrily. "My father was always so encouraging."

"Support yourself and fuck everyone else," Raven snapped.

"Let's talk about something else before I really get depressed," I replied.

"It's good to talk about it, because if you hold it in, you will continue to be angry and bitter. You know how you get," Raven said.

"You're right," I agreed, but still wanting to change the subject, I asked, "So when are we going out?"

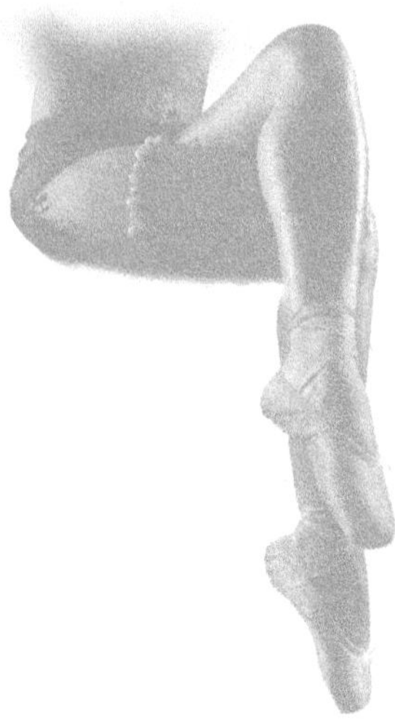

CHAPTER 4

Raven and I were at our favorite reggae club dancing and enjoying the music. The club was crowded and everyone was in their own world enjoying themselves. We always felt free and relaxed at the club because the music made you want to get up and move your body, even if you didn't know how to dance.

When the DJ played a new reggae song that the crowd was not familiar with, everyone stopped dancing and looked at the DJ booth, confused at his choice of song. The song was reggae mixed with a little rhythm and blues.

"I see you looking at me," the DJ yelled into the microphone. "This is a new song by Tank-Rank, and it's rising up the charts fast. Give it a chance and listen."

After listening for a few moments, we immediately started dancing again because the song was great. Raven and I moved our bodies the same way, and everyone always said we looked like identical twins dancing. They didn't know we worked very hard dancing in unison.

We moved like reggae queens on the dance floor, and the crowd made a circle around us to watch our performance. We played with their minds by giving them a dirty show. We danced close on each other and made people gasp for air. For the record, I definitely would not let another girl dance and grind on me, but Raven was special.

"This is the second single from Tank-Rank, and he's in the club tonight," the DJ announced, as he played another song.

We loved Tank-Rank's first single and was happy to hear that he was being consistent with the hits.

As soon as Raven and I got off the dance floor, Tank-Rank's manager approached us and asked if we would be interested in hanging out with him for a day. He explained that he was doing interviews to promote his CD and wanted some beautiful women around him.

We wanted to hear the details because we were very particular about the type of jobs we accepted, but we knew this job would be good networking.

People always told us how beautiful we were, and that we should be modeling and not dancing. Dancing was in our hearts and that was never going to change. However, until our dream job came along, we would continue taking the modeling jobs.

After Raven and I agreed to work with Tank-Rank for the day, his manager handed us his business card and a sheet of paper with the first location he would be visiting.

"Let me introduce you to him," his manager said, than took us over to meet Tank-Rank and his entourage.

Tank-Rank was a down-to-earth guy with a thick Jamaican accent that made it hard to understand him. He looked better in person than on his music videos. His dreadlocks were so long that they touched the lower part of his back, and he wore green, yellow, and red colored clothing.

"I like the way you guys moved to my song. You have talent," he said, while playing with his locks.

"Thanks," we responded in unison.

"I see you're not afraid to dance close to each other," he commented with a smirk.

Raven and I twisted our lips and frowned at him. If Tank-Rank was looking for a freak show, we were not going to be a part of it.

In his thick Jamaican accent, he said, "I'm sorry if I offended you. You guys dance like we do in Jamaica at our rub-a-dub parties, where everyone gets so lost in the music that they start dancing on each other."

We definitely understood what he was saying because that is how we felt when we danced. Dancing did that to us; it made us feel free. No thoughts, no worries, no stress, just freedom.

"I love your look. That's a good combination. A Latino beauty and a black queen," Tank-Rank said staring us.

Raven and I met the executive from his record company, who gave us all the details for the next day. They were going to pay us two hundred and fifty dollars apiece for the day. The record executive told us to dress sexy and look beautiful.

"Tank-Rank will be taking pictures with you, and they will be used in magazines and on his website. You must wear high heel shoes because he loves to hear the sound of heels on the ground. The sound motivates him to write songs," the record executive shared with us.

We looked over the itinerary and saw that his first interview was scheduled for ten o'clock the next morning. From there, we would ride in the limousine with him to the rest of the destinations.

"Don't drive your cars because I don't know where you will end up at the end of the day. Tank-Rank loves to switch things up. Catch a cab to the first location, and we will reimburse you," the record executive said.

We looked at the executive like we didn't believe they would give us our money back. We were used to people in the business not keeping their word. Seeing the look on our face, the executive immediately pulled out one hundred dollars and handed it to us. Raven and I signed the paperwork, and we were hired.

This job would get us closer to dancing on tour with a platinum-selling recording artist. We were willing to put our time in because we knew it would pay off. So, until the big job came along, we would take all the little ones.

~~~~~~~

The next day, we were dressed in tightly-fitted short dresses with four-inch stiletto heels. After putting our make-up on, we were ready for the
~~~~~~~

cameras. We arrived at the first location, which was a record store.

"You girls look beautiful," the record executive said.

We entered the record store and realized they had also hired four other girls. Tank-Rank was signing autographs, taking pictures, and doing interviews, while we catered to him and made him look like a king. We took lots of pictures, and he talked about us to the press like we had been traveling with him for years. Two hours later, we were heading to our next location.

While we were riding in the limousine on our way to a radio station, we were all trying to touchup our make-up.

"Thank you, ladies, for hanging out with me today. I want to get to know you, so tell me your names," Tank-Rank said, then pointed directly at Raven.

"What's up? I'm Raven."

Tank-Rank shouted, "Bullet! Bullet!"

He scared us to death yelling. I was sitting next to Raven, so he pointed at me to give my name.

"Hi, I'm Music."

"Bullet! Bullet!" He shouted loudly again.

He continued to yell after everyone said their names. I had a headache from all the uproar and was getting annoyed. I started frowning, and Raven could feel the tension coming from me.

"Music, fix your face. You know they're all crazy," Raven leaned over and whispered in my ear.

We smiled at each other and joined in with him yelling, "Bullet! Bullet!" This made him more excited, and he started yelling even louder. By the time the last girl said her name, everyone was yelling "Bullet! Bullet!"

"This is what we say in Jamaica when we're excited and like something," Tank-Rank explained.

"Is he going to yell that during sex if he gets excited?" Raven whispered in my ear, as we both started laughing.

After finally arriving at the radio station, we got out of the limousine and started walking toward the entrance.

Tank-Rank said, “Ladies, please stop,” and we immediately obeyed. “Did you hear that?” He asked.

“Hear what?” We asked.

“The sound of beautiful women approaching,” he replied.

We looked at each other confused.

“The sound of your stilettos on the ground drives me wild.”

“This fool is crazy,” I whispered to Raven.

“You know they all have some weird fetish,” she responded.

“Let’s finish this job, get paid, and get the hell away from this nut,” I said, laughing.

For the rest of the day, we made sure he could hear the sound of our heels on the ground. My feet were hurting from walking so hard. I thought to myself since he liked the sound so much, maybe he should put on four-inch stilettos, walk around, and drive himself crazy, because my toes were on fire.

Entertainers are so strange and you never know what makes them tick and what gets their creative juices flowing. I’ve started getting used to people in the music industry being peculiar. Recording artists did whatever they needed to do to get a hit record. They always loved crazy things and had odd requests.

We went to several different places, and according to our itinerary, we had just left our last location. By then, I was ready to go home and soak my feet.

“I’ve enjoyed you guys so much that I don’t want you to leave. I would like for all of you to come to my concert tonight,” Tank-Rank said.

One more step wouldn’t kill me. My feet were already swollen and numb to the point where I didn’t even know I had feet, and Raven’s feet had started to actually bleed. I had warned her not to break in new shoes for this job.

Raven and I laughed at each other and said, "We will not be dancing for at least a week." Our feet needed a break, but the show must go on. So, we continued in pain.

We headed to dinner first and then to Tank-Rank's show, where he introduced us to his band and the rest of his crew backstage.

The show started, and we watched Tank-Rank perform from the side of the stage. Jamaicans knew how to dance and move their pelvic area. We were amazed at how great his show was and how good his music sounded. We definitely were going to buy his new album.

Towards the end of the show, he invited all of us on stage and introduced us to the audience. None of us were thinking about our feet hurting at this time. Our adrenaline kicked in, and we didn't feel a thing.

The band continued to play and everyone started dancing. Raven and I got wrapped up in the music. We were dancing very closely to Tank-Rank and closed him in like a sandwich. Once we snapped back to reality, we had to catch ourselves and back off of him.

"Where are you two going?" He said into the microphone. "You have great talent, the way you move your body. Now let me show you how to do it right."

We were embarrassed because now everyone was looking at us and we thought we were working it, but apparently not.

Tank-Rank grabbed my waist from behind and started moving my hips. He had so much passion in his dancing that I could feel the energy coming from him. The way he was moving my waist made me move to the music much better. My movement was now fluid.

He whispered in my ear, "Don't move to the music. Let the music move you."

The rest of the girls joined us while we partied on stage, and the crowd loved it. When the show was over, we all hung out backstage.

"Are you two professional dancers?" Tank-Rank asked us.

"Yes, we are," Raven quickly answered.

"I would love for you ladies to dance on my tour, but I do most of my shows in Jamaica. I only visit the States a few times a year."

"The next time you're here, look us up and we'll be happy to dance for you," Raven told him.

"Great!" Tank-Rank said, excited.

"When you grabbed my waist on stage, I really felt the moves better," I told Tank-Rank.

"Dance from your soul and feel the music. If you allow the music to move you, you will be an even more amazing dancer," he replied, while moving his hips.

"Thanks. I can really feel the difference," I said, as I joined in moving my hips.

"Most dancers don't dance from their souls. They just do the moves," he added.

"That's why my mother nicknamed me Music. She said whenever I heard any type of music playing I danced and went into a trance."

Tank-Rank quickly grabbed my waist again and said, "This is your center, your pelvic area. In Jamaica, you must know how to move this area well, or people will say you can't dance. This is how I was taught, and I will share it with you. This is the best way to feel the movement and enjoy it."

Tank-Rank showed us how to move our pelvic and told us how important it was. His band members joined in on holding the other girls waists and teaching them to move. Surprisingly, with all the gyrating going on, none of them tried to get fresh with us. They were extremely respectable and professional. By the end of the night, I was moving like a real Jamaican queen.

"You guys have talent. Never give it up," Tank-Rank said.

Raven and I vowed to continue practicing everything he showed us and I will start using it in my choreography. Thanks to Tank-Rank, we would be much better performers. With all the competition, we were happy to find another skill that would separate us from other dancers.

The audience was chanting "encore" and Tank-Rank didn't want to disappoint his fans, so he ran back on stage and invite us to join him. We didn't waste any time for another chance to dance.

We were all having a good time, when Tank-Rank started jumping up and down, which encouraged us to join him. We sung along to his songs and continued to party.

Enjoying the impromptu party on stage, we didn't notice the stage lights over our heads shaking uncontrollably. We kept dancing when all of a sudden the large light came crashing down hitting two of the girls and knocking them completely out.

The glass from the light shattered, almost cutting everyone on stage. Raven and I had pieces of glass in our hair and our legs were bleeding. Tank-Rank and the other girls had minor cuts and none of his band members were injured.

The music stopped and people were in shock. We tried to attend to the girls and waited by their side until the ambulance came. The Paramedics took the two unconscious girls out on stretchers and we were happy we were not joining them.

It was once a party and now it was a tragedy. It's funny how quickly things take a turn for the worse. Tank-Rank was torn up over what happened and stayed as long as he could to see how the girls were doing.

Unfortunately a few days later, one of the girls passed away from head trauma and the other girl was paralyzed. This traumatized dancers everywhere and made us more paranoid to perform on stage.

Raven and I counted our blessings and knew our dreams could have been cut short that night. We promised to live our lives to the fullest and keep striving to live our dreams, enjoying every step and every moment.

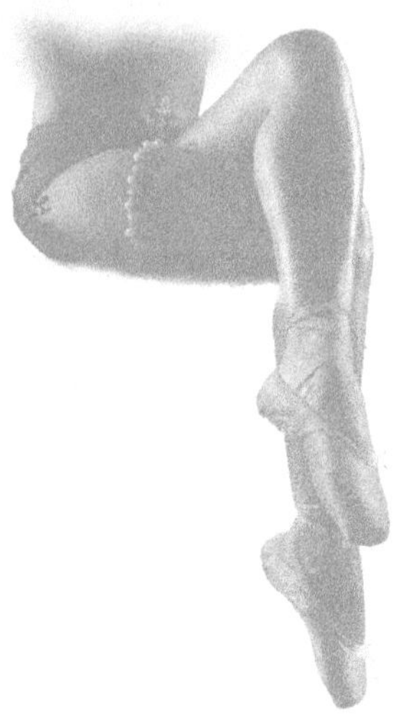

CHAPTER 5

"Good morning, PPC Marketing," I said, answering the telephone at work professionally.

Since things had slowed down, Raven and I were doing shows only once a month and weren't making enough money to quit our jobs, so, we were back at work.

"Guess who we're going to be dancing for?" Raven screamed in the telephone.

"Who?" I whispered so my co-workers didn't hear me.

"We're dancing for Explosion at their concert tonight. They hired us to be the opening act," Raven said, still screaming.

Explosion was a popular male group whose CD was number one. They were known for their harmony, elaborate shows, and unique dance moves. They always hired dancers in every city they performed in to be the opening act. Dancers were waiting all over the world to get their chance to work with them.

"How did you hook that up?" I asked, excited.

"My uncle is friends with the promoter of the show, and he told him about us. He also got us front-row seats, too."

"I can't believe this. What time is the show?"

"It's at seven o'clock and sound check is at five."

"Tonight?"

"Yes, and we have to rehearse and meet the promoter at two o'clock today," Raven replied, while I screamed quietly into the telephone.

"Raven, how am I going to get out of work?"

"I don't know, but you better figure something out fast. I even called the old members from the group. Everyone is excited and available. You can't miss this show," she stressed.

"Let's think of a plan, and I'll call you back in a few minutes," I told her, then hung up.

It was already ten o'clock in the morning, and I needed to leave work, go home to get ready, and meet Raven on time. I didn't want to say I was sick because my boss was extremely strict. He didn't care if you were sick or dying. If you wanted your job, you needed to be working.

I was a secretary for the company and had been there for three years. The office was beautiful with leather couches, large flat-screen televisions, marble floors, and fresh flowers delivered daily.

However, the company was not my type of environment because everyone was always uptight, but I dealt with my co-workers for eight hours a day, five days a week. Still, if it meant I had to wear my business suit and heels to get my paycheck, that's what I did.

I had my own apartment, car, and was doing well for myself. I wasn't rich, not even close, but was happy to be paying my own way through life. The dance jobs gave me plenty of extra money to play around with.

My company didn't believe in employees missing days from work. They gave you sick days, but they didn't expect you to use them. I didn't understand the corporate world. *Why give me something I can't use*?

I never called off sick or took vacation time. All my days were saved just in case I had out-of-town shows. If my boss was going to allow me to leave work early today, I had to come up with something very serious.

I started work at 9:00 a.m., and it was now 10:30 a.m. I needed to leave no later than 12:30 p.m. to be on time for rehearsal. I was too old to be making up elaborate stories just to get out of work, but in this case, I made an exception.

I called Raven back, and after going over different options — well, basically just different lies — Raven came up with a great plan.

"I've got it," Raven said.

"You know it has to be good for it to work."

"Music, go to the bathroom and wait for five minutes. I'll call your job and tell the receptionist that I need to speak with you because your mother had a heart attack. They have to let you leave work early then," she said.

"Raven, that's perfect. Who would deny me from going to see my mother in the hospital?" I said excitedly.

"You can't miss this show," Raven stated again.

"Wait fifteen minutes before you make the call. That will give me time to get myself together and go to the bathroom to wait."

"Okay. Get your acting skills ready. Don't mess this up, Music."

"I won't. Let's do it."

I went to the bathroom and played in my hair trying to waste time. About five minutes later, two of my co-workers walked in and stood there watching me for a few moments with a strange look on their face.

"Why are you looking at me like that?" I asked.

"Music, you need to go back to the office immediately," they said simultaneously.

"Why?"

"Your mother had a heart attack," they said in unison.

That was the time for me to give my Oscar award-winning performance and act like I was in total shock.

"Oh God!" I kept saying, while tears started forming in my eyes.

I rushed out of the bathroom crying and shaking, but on the inside I was smiling because I knew the plan was working. As I walked into the office, everyone kept asking me if I'd heard about my mother as I passed by. I thought to myself, *Damn, news travels fast.*

"I'm on my way to the hospital," I told them.

Since everyone knew what was going on, I knew it would not be a problem for me to leave early now. I rushed to my desk, grabbed my coat, and headed towards my boss's office to let him know I was leaving. He had to have heard about my mother by now.

When I rushed to his office, he was on the telephone and put his index finger up in the air, signaling for me to wait outside his door. His telephone call was taking long and I started getting nervous.

Once he finished the call, he immediately jumped up out of his chair, grabbed his coat, and came running out of his office.

"Your mother had a heart attack. We have to get to the hospital now!" He said, as I stood there stunned. I didn't expect him to go with me. I had to think fast.

"My cousin is picking me up and we're going to go to the hospital together," I told him nervously.

I couldn't think of any other lie. He stared at me for what seemed like hours but was only a few seconds. I'm not sure whether he believed me, thought I didn't want him to go, or if he genuinely wanted to be there for me. This awkward moment was taking way too long.

Still shaking and with tears running down my cheeks, I shouted, "I have to go! My mother might die!"

I'm not sure why I said that, but desperation came out of me.

"You should leave now," he said, then added, "I'll pray for your mother."

His comment hit me hard. Why did he have to be so nice and concerned? Who told him to come with me anyway? He was usually mean, uptight, and didn't care about anyone. He was making it very difficult for me.

I rushed out of the office and didn't stop running until I reached the train. It was 12:25 p.m., five minutes ahead of schedule. I felt terrible about lying to my boss and co-workers, but I would get over it.

I was on my way to dance for the group Explosion and see their show in front-row seats. Therefore, it was worth it. Dancing meant so much to me that I was willing to risk getting fired. I was determined not to let anything get in my way of achieving my goals.

~~~~~~~

Our performance for Explosion's show went great; the crowd loved us and gave us a standing ovation. Once we were done performing, we were ready to watch the show in our front row seats.

During intermission, we walked into a packed and very noisy lobby of the sold-out concert. Everyone was talking about how great the concert was and naming their favorite member.

I loved all of the members of the group, but Ken and Tim were my favorites. Ken seemed like the good boy that would be good to you and love you always. Tim seemed like the bad boy that would definitely do you wrong every time, but of course, Tim was the type of guy that the girls went for, and I was no different.

People were doing Explosion dance steps right in the middle of the lobby. I looked at them and laughed at how crazy they looked messing up the dance routines. Like the back of my hand, I knew all of the choreography. Studying their music videos helped me do their moves effortlessly. Dancing was my God-given talent, and I could pick up on any step quicker than any of my friends.

The first time I was paid to dance in a show was an eye opener. Making money dancing, while not required to take my clothes off, was confirmation of what my new occupation would be.

The crowd was buying food, standing in line for the restrooms, and buying Explosion tour books and t-shirts. I went straight for the tour book line, while everyone else was trying to decide what to do first before the short intermission ended.
~~~~~~~

I couldn't wait to get the tour book and read all the exciting information. It had pictures of the group and dancers, upcoming tour dates, and fan club information. It also showed pictures of the tour bus and had behind-the-scene shots of the concerts.

Amazed at how many people it took to put a tour together, it made me dream of going on the road and seeing my name and picture in a tour book someday. I wondered what life on the road would be like and wanted to know how it felt to live on a tour bus for months while traveling around the world.

Seeing pictures of the dancers laughing with the artists and the band goofing around really made me want to be a part of that life. The tour book served its purpose of making me feel closer to the entertainer and their entourage.

Intermission was over and the show as starting. Explosion was on the stage by the time we reached our seats, which were front and center. After the concert, we got our tour books signed and met Explosion.

We even hung out with them and took lots of pictures. Being able to meet and talk to Explosion made them feel real to me. They didn't seem like people who only existed on television.

While we were sitting around backstage laughing and talking, Raven was flirting with some of the men and even exchanged numbers with a few of them. She quickly pointed out to me that she thought James was gay, and she was going to make her move.

Girls were lined up outside of Tim's dressing room waiting to see him. We met him briefly, but after he realized we were not there to be his sex toys for the night, he quickly pushed us to the side to get to the girls that were waiting, willing and ready.

I wished we never met Tim because he was no longer appealing to us and didn't deserve any respect because he was rude. I just wanted to keep the same feelings I had for him before we met, but unfortunately those feelings went down the drain.

Raven and I left the concert with larger than life smiles on our faces. I left the concert wanting to go on tour more than ever. Not wanting to see Explosion get on the tour bus and leave without me, it turned out to be a bittersweet night.

~~~~~~~

I loved reading magazines to catch up on all the latest news and gossip of my favorite entertainer on tour. I always dreamed of being on the road with them to enjoy the same fun they appeared to be having throughout the pages of the magazine.

I wanted to be a part of their entourage, and like millions of other people, I dreamed of having the life of the rich and famous. Reading interviews of entertainers talking about where they've traveled and where they were appearing next, made me want to pack my bags and get on the next airplane with them.

Entertainers didn't seem like real people to the average person. All the glamour and fame made them seem untouchable.

I've always been told that the music industry was corrupted. It made good girls go wild and good boys go crazy. I've always heard that you had to sleep your way to the top if you wanted to make it, but I only thought that was true if I wanted to be an actress. I didn't know that was the same for dancers.

I believed I could make it on my talent alone. I wasn't going to spread my legs to become successful. I was going to prove everyone wrong, especially my mom who didn't want me anywhere near this business.

People would do anything to be rich and famous. They say there is always a price to pay for fame. I was determined to successfully enter the music industry pure and innocent and remain that way.

Until I reached my goal of going on a world tour with a famous entertainer, I would continue dancing for local artists. All the small gigs had to pay off soon.

In this business, I knew it was all about networking, and each show I did put me that much closer to the big one. It was only a matter of time.
~~~~~~~

CHAPTER 6

Raven and I were dancing for a new recording artist named London, and this was our first time traveling to New Orleans to perform. London's song was getting tons of radio play, and her first single had been number one on the charts for weeks.

She was a hard worker and very dedicated to her career. She was well on her way to becoming a platinum-selling artist. Her second single had just hit the number one spot and she wanted to celebrate.

After the last show, London took me, Raven, her manager Troy, the band members, and crew out to celebrate. We went to Bourbon Street, which was the best place in New Orleans to celebrate her success. Bourbon Street had tons of bars, and it was where tourists went for fun. The street was crowded, everyone was happily drunk, and this set the mood off right for us. We were excited and wanted to have a good time.

This celebration was very important for all of us. For London, it meant making more money and becoming a well-known singer. For Raven and me, it meant more shows and more cash.

With different types of music ringing in the air, people were pouring out of the bars dancing, drinking, and laughing. It was so crowded that people were bumping into each other. If you were in a bad mood, it wouldn't last long. If you didn't drink alcohol, you wanted to start.

Watching people have so much fun made you want to join them. We danced down the street like we were on stage. We laughed and spoke to every stranger we saw.

We stopped at the first bar to drink and celebrate. As soon as we walked into the establishment, we shouted out, "We're celebrating London's second number one hit!"

The entire bar clapped and joined us in the celebration. There were several people who recognized London and asked for an autograph.

"Congratulations on your number one song. I'm going to make you guys a special drink," the bartender told us.

He introduced us to a drink called Poppers and gave us special instructions on how to drink it. We covered the top of the drink with our hand, picked up the glass, and hit the glass on the table three times until it fizzed up. Then we drank it straight down.

I hated the taste of liquor, but I was there to celebrate. So, I drank it. The faster I drank, the more I didn't taste the alcohol.

"Music, you can't hang with us," London kept saying, while laughing.

"I'm going to hang with you guys tonight," I replied, as I kept drinking.

I never believed my friends when they admitted to being so drunk that they blacked out and couldn't remember anything. I didn't understand how alcohol could do that to someone. I never drank so much alcohol before than I did tonight, and now I understand the meaning of being pissy drunk.

"Why are you trying to drink so much? Music, you need to slow down," Raven kept telling me all night.

"Don't worry about me. I can handle it," I said.

Even though I wasn't sure what I was doing, I wanted to try something different and do something out of my character for a change. I never liked consuming a lot of alcohol because I didn't think women looked sexy drunk. Falling all over the place, talking loud or crying was not lady like.

I was comfortable knowing that Raven wouldn't let me do anything to embarrass myself, and I trusted her with my life. I was going to join in the celebration with everyone by drinking heavily and enjoying the night.

We went to almost every bar on Bourbon Street, drinking two to three Poppers per bar. The last place was a gay cabaret bar, where the men were dressed up like women. Heterosexual men usually freaked out about being in a gay bar, but the band members and crew were so drunk that they didn't even care.

Being a heterosexual woman, I was secure with my sexuality. Being in a gay bar didn't bother London or me. However, Raven felt right at home.

We laughed at some of the ugly men dressed up like women. Some of them made absolutely beautiful women, and some should never put on women clothing again.

"Music, this is the last one. You can finish it," London and Raven said, while holding the glass up to my mouth.

"I've had enough. I can't take another sip," I told them in a drunken stupor.

We were drinking our last Popper for the night, but my body could not handle any more liquor. The gay men kept encouraging me to keep drinking by yelling, "Take that bitch to the head." Everyone was cheering me on to finish my drink, so I did.

"It's time to go," I said, while stumbling to the door.

The liquor had set in, and I was officially drunk. No longer in control of my body, I couldn't walk straight. This was definitely not the look I wanted. I was ready to leave quickly before embarrassing myself.

We left the bar and started walking towards the hotel a few blocks away. I remembered leaving the bar, but I didn't remember walking to the hotel. I became alert once we reached the hotel entrance.

Everyone who performed with us on the show was staying at the same hotel. Not wanting people to know I was drunk, I tried to stand up straight and walk without falling over.

Raven was also drunk, but was able to keep her composure. There were a few dancers on the elevator when we got on, and we could not hide the fact that we had been drinking because the smell of liquor was seeping out of our pores.

"What's up Raven?" Daniel asked.

"Nothing much," she responded.

"What are you guys getting into tonight?" He inquired.

"Our night is over. We're going to our room to relax," Raven said, as she stared at Daniel, who was a dancer who performed on the show with us.

Raven was infatuated by him and the feelings seemed to be mutual. Raven and Daniel met at the airport as soon as we arrived in New Orleans. They exchanged telephone numbers and had been talking on the telephone the entire time we've been here.

"This is our floor. I'll talk to you later," Raven told Daniel flirtatiously, as we got off the elevator. When Daniel smiled and winked at her, Raven melted inside.

London and her manager Troy followed us to the room Raven and I shared. We were not staying at a five-star hotel, but the rooms were clean. Our small room was decorated with floral prints. The couch and chair had the same floral print as the curtains. Both beds had comforters that also had the same horrible floral print.

There was a dresser with a large television on it and one nightstand in between the beds. Whoever designed the rooms went a little overboard with the floral print and was making us feel like we were in a garden.

As soon as we walked into our hotel room, we headed straight for the beds to lie down. A few minutes later, everyone but Troy was vomiting all over the bed and floor. We were too drunk to clean it up, so Troy covered the vomit with towels, and the smell smothered the room instantly.

"Get up, London. I got to get you to your room," Troy said, helping her off the bed. "Once London is settled, I will be back to check on you guys," he said, while guiding London to the door.

London couldn't make it out of the room without vomiting on the floor again, and Troy knew he had to get to her room fast. He didn't want anyone to see her in this condition because it was not good for her image. Being a new recording artist, she didn't need any bad publicity. Effortlessly, Troy picked her up and walked out of the room.

Whenever I leaned over towards the floor to vomit, I hit my head on the nightstand and then hit it again when I lifted my head back up. Raven was trying to help me, but she kept vomiting, too.

I was so drained that I couldn't do anything but lay on the bed in a stiff fetal position. By this time, our hotel room was destroyed and smelled awful. There was no doubt we were going to get charged for the cleaning.

Raven kept walking around, because the moment she stopped moving, the room started spinning. In an attempt to comfort me, she put a wet towel on my head, when she heard a knock at the door.

"I came to check on you guys since you seemed pretty hammered on the elevator," Daniel told Raven, with a concerned look on his face.

"Thanks for checking on us, but we're doing fine," Raven said, while blushing.

"Are you going to let me in or do I have to talk to you in from hallway?" He asked. Raven was hesitant to allow him in the room because of my condition and the odor.

"Sure, come in," she said reluctantly.

Raven opened the door wider to let him in, and then she immediately came back to the bed and sat down beside me. Daniel didn't seem to mind the strong smell of vomit in the room, or at least he never said anything about it.

One look at Daniel and Raven was immediately turned on. He was 6'1" with a muscular body, perfectly white teeth, beautiful green eyes, wavy black hair and spoke with a London accent that sent chills throughout her body. Raven didn't care if she was drunk or if our room reeked of puke. She just wanted to be around him.

Daniel sat next to Raven and me on the bed, and they talked while she rubbed my forehead with a cold towel. I was feeling much better, but really didn't have any strength to move. So, I closed my eyes and went to sleep.

I woke up thirty minutes later, and they were still talking, when I started feeling someone caress my thigh. The hand moved from my thigh to my butt, where it continued to rub. The hand moved and started rubbing me aggressively between my legs. I thought this was weird because Raven knew I didn't swing that way and neither did she.

When I opened my eyes, I saw that one of Raven's hands was rubbing my forehead and her other hand was on her lap. I knew then that it was Daniel touching me. I was so drained I couldn't move or talk. All I could do was moan.

"What's wrong?" Raven kept asking me. "Relax."

With the sound of me moaning and Raven's concern, Daniel stopped touching me.

Before I passed out again, I saw Raven, who was exhausted, lay back on the bed next to me. I fell asleep wondering if Daniel knew Raven was a man. Since he was just rubbing on my butt, I didn't think he was gay.

I woke up trying to change position from the curled-up position I was in, when I saw Daniel climbing on top of Raven with his dick in his hand. He pulled her skirt up, lifted both of her legs in the air, and plunged his dick in her asshole.

I couldn't believe Raven would have sex next to me in the same bed. Sure, she was my best friend and we did everything together, but this was where I drew the line.

I noticed that Raven's body was lifeless, and the only person pumping like a dog in heat was Daniel. Since I couldn't move or say anything, I closed my eyes and quickly fell asleep again.

It seemed like hours had passed, but I was only asleep for twenty minutes. I woke up and Daniel was climbing off of Raven and immediately moved over to me. He tried to get my pants off, but my body was in a locked position, stopping him.

"Stop," I said in a weak voice.

He quickly stopped and jumped up off the bed. He went to the telephone that was on the dresser and made a call.

"Hey man, come to room 510 right now," Daniel told someone on the other end of the telephone.

After hanging up, he went straight to the bathroom. I assumed he was going to wash his dick off since he didn't use a condom while having sex with Raven.

As soon as the bathroom door closed, I found the strength to get up and quickly call Troy's room.

"Come to our room right now!" I said franticly.

"Music, what's wrong?" Troy asked.

"Just come quickly," I replied and hung up.

While Daniel was in the bathroom, I heard a knock on the door. I opened it, hoping it was Troy, but it was Daniel's dance partner Kevin.

"May I help you?" I asked as soon as I saw him.

Kevin stood in the doorway looking at me and licking his lips. "Where's Daniel?" He asked, as he pushed his way into the room.

"Daniel is in the bathroom. What do you want?"

"I want you," he said, quickly trying to kiss me.

"Stop, what are you doing?" I said, pushing him off of me.

Daniel heard us and came out of the bathroom. They looked at each other with a grin on their faces. Daniel didn't waste any time and grabbed me from behind, pulling me on the bed on top on him. Kevin grabbed my shirt and ripped it open, while Daniel continued to hold me.

I was fighting, but they were so strong it was hard for me to move. Kevin moved quickly, licking my neck and breasts. His hands were frantically rubbing all over my body.

"No! Stop!" I managed to scream before Daniel stopped me.

Daniel was covering my mouth with one hand while using his other hand to try to open my pants. They worked together, and it was obvious they had done this before.

Kevin grabbed my pants and tried to take them off. I was happy I had on tight jeans, because he was struggling to get them off. Raven was still asleep on the bed and didn't hear me fighting with them.

We had been wrestling for a few minutes, when Troy ran into the room and pulled Kevin off of me, throwing him on the floor. Thank God the door was unlocked. He pushed me to the side, grabbed Daniel, and punched him in his face. Kevin jumped up and grabbed Troy from behind. That gave Daniel time to get up, and they both started beating him. By then, I was screaming and crying.

"Music, what's going on?" Raven said, finally waking up from all the commotion.

"We got to help Troy!" I screamed at her.

Raven didn't know what was happening, but she saw Troy was in trouble and knew she had to do something. I grabbed a lamp and hit Daniel on the arm. Raven went crazy and jumped on Kevin's back, scratching him in the face.

For Raven to be a man, she was truly fighting like a girl. Daniel swung at me, punching me in the arm, and I fell to the floor.

After getting his momentum, Troy started beating both of them, while Raven and I sat on the floor trying to catch our breath. Finally, Kevin and Daniel managed to run out of the room. I ran behind them and locked the door.

"What the hell happened in here?" Troy asked, out of breathe.

"Daniel and Kevin tried to rape me," I blurted out.

"What?" Raven said, surprised.

I never told them that Daniel raped Raven because I didn't want to embarrass her.

"Let's call the police," Troy said.

"I'm okay. I'm just glad this is over," I told him, as I sat on the bed shaking and crying.

Raven was still sitting on the floor with her mouth hanging open.

"Are you sure you don't want to do anything? They shouldn't get away with this," Troy said angrily.

"It's my word against theirs. No one believes a woman when it has something to do with sex. The man tells everyone the woman is a whore and people believe him. The woman always turns out to be the bad person. I've seen it happen too many times, and I don't feel like fighting that battle," I replied sadly.

"I'll be your witness," Troy said.

"Let's just forget about it. I'll be fine," I said.

"Okay, if that's what you want to do," he replied.

"I'm so mad I want to kill them. I just don't feel like going through any drama," I said, while wiping the tears from my eyes.

"Are you really okay?" Raven asked, concerned.

"I'm good," I told her.

Raven seemed embarrassed for me, so she never asked what happened.

"Music, you shouldn't let them get away with this. You always let people treat you wrong." Raven said, frustrated.

"I'm not as strong as you. Besides, they didn't actually rape me," I responded.

"Just because they didn't rape you, don't mean they should get away with it. You really need to get some balls," she said.

I looked at Raven when she said balls, because she had enough for the both of us.

"They only did this because we were drunk," I stated.

"Well, no more drinking for us." Raven said.

"Get your stuff together because we will be leaving in a few hours," Troy said, annoyed.

We had a few hours before our flight, and we made it on time to the airport. We still felt drunk and could barely make it to the check-in counter without feeling like we were going to faint. We managed to get through the check-in process and then to the gate to catch our flight.

"Hello and welcome," the flight attendant greeted us as we boarded the plane.

"Can we have some bottles of water?" I immediately asked.

"You will have to wait until the flight starts," she replied.

"We're sick, so could you please get us something to drink?" Raven asked.

"I said you have to wait," the flight attendant responded rudely.

"Look, you either get us something to drink or we're going to barf all over these damn seats," Raven said aggressively.

The flight attendant rolled her eyes and walked away. A few moments later, she returned with two bottles of water, and five minutes later, the pilot was standing at our seats.

"Hello, ladies. Are you okay?" The pilot asked us.

"Yes," Raven told him.

"Are you guys sick, or did you enjoy yourself too much last night in New Orleans?" The pilot asked with a smile on his face.

"We enjoyed ourselves a little too much," I replied.

"I wanted to make sure we wouldn't have any issues once we were up in the air," the pilot said, quite relieved.

Raven and I slept the entire flight and made it home safely. Our lesson for life was being drunk is dangerous and will get you in serious trouble.

~~~~~~

A few weeks had past, and we were on our way to do another show for the singer London. Since her record sells were going great, she sent a limousine to take us to the show.
~~~~~~

I had not had a drink since New Orleans and was determined to never let alcohol touch these lips again. I was still traumatized by the incident, but I kept moving and wasn't going to let it stop me.

"Are you ready to put it down tonight?" I asked Raven, while putting on more lip gloss.

"Yeah, I'm ready," Raven said nonchalantly.

She seemed really distant and not herself. Usually on the way to our shows, we were always talking and laughing, but this time it was different.

"What's wrong with you, girl?" I jokingly said, while pushing her in the arm.

"Nothing, I'm cool," Raven responded in the same nonchalant manner.

"I know when something is wrong with you, and you're not acting right. What's up?" I asked, demanding an explanation.

"I said I'm cool. Now leave me alone," she said, this time with an attitude.

"We had a couple of weeks off since the New Orleans show, so I know you're not still drunk and tired. Girl, we have a show in an hour, and I need you to be one hundred percent on point. You can talk to me about anything; I'm your girl. Now what the hell is wrong with you, bitch?" I said seriously.

This made Raven laughed.

"Bitch! I see you've learned a new word."

"That's the only word I know you can understand and will respond to."

"I got a sexually transmitted disease, and I'm not sure who I got it from," Raven blurted out, as she tried to stop the tears from running down her face.

"Damn, Raven, how many men are you sleeping with that you don't remember?" I asked teasingly, oblivious that she was hurt.

She started crying.

"Raven, I'm sorry. I didn't know you were serious," I said, while handing her some tissue.

"I don't know how I got a STD, and I would remember having sex with someone. I feel like I'm going crazy," Raven said, totally confused.

She was torn up about this and couldn't stop crying. While trying to comfort her, I thought about what happened in New Orleans with Daniel. I was contemplating if I should tell her, but I didn't want to hurt her.

Raven never talked to me about the night in the hotel room, and I never told her what I saw. She only knew that Daniel and Kevin tried to rape me. Now that she was telling me this, I knew she didn't know Daniel had raped her.

Raven kept crying, and I felt so bad that I decided to tell her what happened. I wanted her to have a peace of mind instead of wondering.

"Raven, I need to tell you something," I said with tears now in my eyes.

"What's wrong with you?" She asked.

"Just listen," I told her.

She was in shock while I explained to her what Daniel had done to her.

"Music, stop lying. I just spoke with Daniel."

"Raven, I wouldn't lie about something so serious. He's a rapist, and he tried to rape me."

"You have an unexplained STD. You know I wouldn't make up a story like this."

Raven continued to stare at me, trying to understand everything.

"My asshole has been sore ever since we came from New Orleans. My whole body has been aching, too. I thought it was because of all the liquor we drank," she said.

"I'm sorry. I know you really like Daniel. I didn't tell you because I didn't want to embarrass you. I'm so sorry."

"You should have told me. You supposed to be my girl and have my back," Raven said furious. "That bastard called me this morning asking me to fly to London to see him. I'm going to make his ass pay for this."

"I'm so sorry. Are you going to be okay?"

"I'm going to be fine. That just messed me up. But, it's not like I've never been screwed in my ass before. I just would've wanted to be awake so I could have enjoyed him, and of course, I would have covered up his dirty dick with a condom," Raven said, trying to crack a joke.

We both laughed.

"Did you know Daniel was gay?" I asked her.

"Yes, I knew he was gay. I can spot them anywhere," she replied.

"Do you think Daniel will tell people you're a man?" I asked with concern.

"He won't tell because people don't know he's gay. He has a lot to lose just like me if word got out about us," she said with confidence.

"I would be terrified that he would tell your secret."

"Girl, unless he goes straight, he won't say anything."

Raven didn't like me talking about her being a man. She wanted me to act like she was a natural woman. I was still traumatized from seeing her getting fucked in her ass, and she was trying to act nonchalant about the incident, but it was obvious she was really distressed.

The show went great and Raven gave me the energy I was looking for. She definitely knew how to put her personal life to the side and perform. One thing you learn is to never bring your problems on stage.

London's show was a hit, and her manager was talking about more shows in the future. Raven gathered her belongings and quickly went to the limousine, waiting to go home. I followed behind her.

"I think I'm going to take a break from this crazy music industry," she said very seriously.

"Raven, why?"

"That New Orleans trip got my mind messed up."

"That could've happened anywhere. Please don't stop dancing. We're on our way to making it big," I pleaded with her.

"Give me some time to get over this."

"I'm sorry I didn't tell you, Raven. I was only trying to protect you. I didn't want to hurt you."

"Just give me a break for now. I need some time."

"How long of a break do you need?"

"Just give me some damn time." Raven yelled as she looked at me irately.

"If that's what you need, then I'll give you some space," I responded sadly.

"I can't believe Daniel did that to me. I don't know what I'm feeling."

"I understand. I'm here if you need to talk."

"Don't get too comfortable. I won't be gone long."

"Good because I can't dance without you. Are you still going to the audition next month?" I asked her.

"No, I think I'll sit this one out, but I'll be ready for the next one. You go and represent for the both of us."

"What are you going to be doing?"

"I'm going to switch things up for a while and do some modeling to keep my mind off of this."

"I don't want to go to the audition, if you're not going."

"Go to the audition. I'll be fine."

"It won't be the same without you."

"I know it won't," Raven said, as we both laughed.

CHAPTER 7

“What’s up, Shorty?” Que said, excited.

“Hey, big brother, what are you up to stranger?” I said.

“I was calling because my group is shooting a video and I want you to be in it. Are you available next week?”

“I’m available. You know I wouldn’t miss your video,” I said happy that he thought about me. I hadn’t spoken to Que in a while and it was nice to hear his voice again.

“I also want you to dance on our tour,” Que said.

“Of course I will. The family will be together. Thanks for thinking of me.”

“I know I’ve been busy and haven’t been in contact with you, but I’ve been out here trying to get this paper. You know I’m going to look out for you. That’s why I’m calling you.”

“Can my dance partner Raven be in the video?” I asked.

“It’s cool, just as long as she’s beautiful.”

“Trust me, you won’t be disappointed.”

“Bring your girl with you. Tell your mother I said hello,” he said.

“When I talk to her, I will.”

“She’s still not supporting your dance career?” Que asked.

"No. She doesn't want me in the music business. She hates it," I replied.

"Well, she has no choice but to deal with it because you're all up in it," Que said, laughing.

"I'm going to keep moving on with or without her support."

"She'll come around."

"Who cares?" I said quickly.

"My manager will call you with all the details. See you at the video shoot," Que said.

Que was the singer of the group Destruction, and Sean and James were the rappers. Que had a light caramel complexion, and Sean and James were light-skinned, very muscular, and gorgeous.

When Que and I were younger, we always dreamed of becoming rich and famous, and we were now proud of each other's success. Most people didn't understand our close friendship.

He was like a brother to me and we would do anything for each other. I was the sister he never had, and he was the brother I've always wanted. We really believed we were family and always treated each other that way.

I called Raven hoping she was available to shoot the video with me. She had been busy modeling and was hired to be the spokes model for a clothing line.

"I wish I could do the video, but I have a photo shoot that day," Raven said.

"You're never available anymore. Do you still want to dance?" I asked.

"Yes, I still love dancing, but modeling is very good to me right now and I have to keep riding this," she said.

"I understand. You're getting very popular in the modeling industry. I'm proud of you, girl."

"Thanks. Now go do the video and show them what you're working with."

"I will, but I will miss you."

"Call me the next day and tell me all about it. Tell Que I said what's up, with his cute ass."

Thrilled to be a part of Que's video shoot, I was at the set bright and early. The video shoot was totally different from Riff Raff's low-budget video. Destruction definitely had a bigger budget. There were trailers, make-up artists, and stylists for the dancers. They also provided breakfast, lunch, snacks, and dinner.

I walked into my plush trailer that had a large flat-screen television, snacks, a make-up room, living room area, and a bedroom with a bathroom and shower. I felt like a rock star and was enjoying the royal treatment.

Once again, I was waiting all day before they were ready to film me. There were three lead girls for the video, and as usual, they were all light-skinned. There were tons of extras and many video vixens on set that were all fighting for the spotlight.

The make-up artist made me look beautiful, and I felt like I was the star of the video. I was dressed in a sexy outfit, ready to perform for the camera.

"Damn, you look beautiful," Que said, as he stuck his head in the door of my trailer.

"Thanks. You don't look bad yourself," I said smiling.

"Are you ready?"

"I'm ready. Thanks again, Que, for hooking me up."

"We're family. You know I was going to lookout for you."

"Thank you."

"Do you have a bottle of water? I need to take my medicine," Que asked.

"It's water in the refrigerator. What's wrong with you? Why are you taking medicine?" I inquired.

"It's nothing. Just some Vicodin I'm taking for my toothache."

"Are you still afraid of the dentist? You need to take care of that."

"I will as soon as I get some time. Thanks for the water."

"No problem."

"I'll see you on set," he said, then walked out, closing the trailer door behind him.

After I walked on set, the director explained that he wanted the lead girls to dance around the group, while the extras and video vixens stayed in the background scene to make it look lively.

Once the cameras started filming us, it seemed like I was getting lost in the background. The video vixens were making their way front and center, pushing me out of the way. I worked extra hard to get some camera time, but no one even noticed me.

Once again, the light-skinned girls were the center of attention. I couldn't believe I was getting treated like this at Que's video shoot. When we took a five-minute break, I went to talk to him.

"Why are all the dark-skinned girls in the background?" I asked.

"You know it's not like that," Que responded.

"You guys need to recognize that black is beautiful," I said, as I playfully hit him.

"Okay, Music. I'm going to talk to the director. I'll take care of it."

"You better," I demanded.

We continued the video shoot, but nothing changed. I couldn't believe Que was treating me this way. He knew how I felt about being treated equally. Still, racism was alive and kicking in the entertainment business.

I was used to not being chosen because of the color of my skin, but it always hurt when it was my own race doing the discriminating.

Since there was no change in filming of the video shoot, I walked off the set and went to get a cup of coffee. Sadly, no one ever noticed that I left.

"This is some bullshit," one of the dancers said to herself, while pouring a cup of coffee.

"Can you pass me the cream?" I asked.

"Why aren't you filming?" She asked me.

"Probably the same reason you're not. Because black is not beautiful to them."

We made our coffee and introduced ourselves to each other.

"I'm tired of not being seen," Mia responded.

We started talking and found out we had a lot in common. Mia complained about how dark-skinned people always got treated differently and how tired she was of the discrimination.

Mia had been in the business for a long time and continued to experience the same rejections I did. We had an instant dancer connection.

"I've seen you at a few auditions before, and you're a great dancer. I know of some upcoming auditions where they love dark-skinned dancers. Do you want to go with me?" Mia asked.

"Sure," I said.

Mia wanted us to take over the dance world and show them how it's really done. She wanted us to dance together. I felt a little uncomfortable at first because it was like she would be taking Raven's place. Raven was busy modeling and it would be nice to have another temporary dance partner, especially since I wasn't sure when Raven would return.

I watched Mia dancing while we were filming the video, and she was great.

"We should be called M and M," I told her.

She loved the idea. Both of our names started with the letter M, and we were chocolate in complexion like the M&M candy. It was perfect. We exchanged numbers and agreed to meet up at the next audition.

When the director saw us sitting in the corner talking and drinking coffee, he walked over to me while they were on break setting up another shot.

"Music, I want you to be in the next scene," the director said.

Que immediately walked over and grabbed me. "I told you that I would take care of it. Now come on and do this scene with me, my little chocolate drop."

"Oh, now you want some chocolate in your life?" I said laughing.

For the scene, I sat on the couch next to Destruction, while they performed their song. I was the only dark-skinned girl in the shot, and I definitely stood out. When we finished filming, a photographer took pictures and it became the cover for Destruction's CD.

I was happy I got a little camera time but I was still upset about the way I was treated. The only reason I was in that shot was because I complained to Que about not being seen, and knowing the artist and getting the hook up seemed to be the only way I was going to advance in this business.

I was so tired of working extra hard, but that's how the entertainment industry is; either I get with the program or get out of the business.

Once the video shoot was over, Mia gave me the audition information for the female group called Lipstick. *Here's to a new friendship and more jobs,* I thought to myself.

"Que, I will talk to you soon," I told him.

"You better call me," Que said, then popped another pill in his mouth and washed it down with water.

"Are you taking more Vicodin?" I asked.

"Yeah, my tooth is killing me."

"Que, you really need to go to the dentist. It's not good to keep popping those pills."

"Yes, mother. I'm going to take care of it," Que replied sarcastically.

"You better," I said, then hugged him goodbye.

~~~~~~~

"Are you ready for the audition?" Mia asked as soon as I answered the telephone.

"Girl, you know I am. Thanks for hooking me up."

"Thank me when we get the job."
~~~~~~~

The group Lipstick was only looking for two dancers, and of course, we wanted them to hire us. We came up with a plan to get them to see us dancing together. We rehearsed at Mia's apartment to create a routine for the audition.

Mia had a large loft apartment with lots of room for dancing. I was amazed at how talented she was. She had the same drive as me, and she loved dancing and choreographing as much as I did.

We were both quick learners, which made the rehearsals much easier. We made sure the routine showed all of our special talents. We added turns, jumps, kicks, and mixed in some reggae moves. We worked great together and looked amazing.

I was pleasantly shocked that someone other than Raven could catch on to my unique dance steps and do them so easy. We were so much alike, it was scary. After rehearsing for a couple of days, we were definitely ready.

I met Mia in front of the club where the auditions were being held. We waited outside to see some of the other dancers. We wanted to see our competition. We finally entered the club, but waited to sign in.

We wanted to make sure we were the last two dancers auditioning. They always made you audition separately, but we were a package and wanted to audition together.

Just as planned, we were the last two dancers on the list. They called my name first. Immediately, we both stood up and walked on the stage ready to audition.

I gave them my name and said, "We would like to audition together. If you don't like us, then we can audition separately. I think you will be pleased."

At first, the group Lipstick and their entourage looked like they were annoyed by our act. However, once I kept going on with my pleading, they gave us a chance.

One of the group's members warned us, "You better make it good."

They played the song and we ripped the stage. Once we were done, one of the members of the group said, "Wow, you guys are great. Can you wait around for a moment while we make our decision?"

"Sure," Mia and I replied in unison.

About ten minutes later, they told us we were hired.

"Be ready for rehearsal tomorrow and bring those moves you guys were doing on stage. The show is next week," a member of the group said.

"How much is the job paying?" Mia quickly asked.

"Each dancer will get paid two hundred and fifty dollars for the show."

"What about pay for the rehearsals?" Mia asked.

I was not used to getting paid for rehearsals. So, any pay was good for me.

"We pay the dancers seventy-five dollars a day for rehearsals."

"Thanks. I wanted to make sure we were able to accept the job. We're happy to be working with you. See you tomorrow," Mia replied in a business tone.

We walked out of that audition satisfied.

"What made you ask them to pay us for rehearsals?" I asked her.

"In this business, you shouldn't do anything for free, and you should always get paid for rehearsals. Most dancers don't ask questions about payment and accept whatever pay they're offered because they're just happy to get hired. If you don't demand to get paid, they will never pay you."

Mia's advice was to never dance for free and to demand respect. I never thought about the respect of it. I never requested pay or challenged the pay rate. The industry needed to respect us like they did everyone else, and doing things for free didn't help.

I felt bad because all this time I was trying to help dancers make it in the business, but I was missing a very important part which was respect.

Mia continued schooling me on the entertainment business, and after talking with her, I realized there was a lot I needed to learn. I listened and soaked up the information like a sponge, and afterwards, I had a new outlook.

The next day, we started rehearsals. Lipstick was an all-female R&B meets rock group, and they allowed us to choreograph and develop their whole show. We put together a cool show, creating a difficult chair routine.

Our outfits for the show were short black skirts, thigh high black patent leather boots and black fitted tops. The group wore the same outfit, but in all red. Everyone was prepared to have a great show.

A week passed and we were at the club performing. The crowd loved Lipstick, and after the second song, they left the stage for a quick wardrobe change. While they were offstage, Mia and I did our chair routine.

We did high kicks over the chair, jumped, and stood up on them. The crowd seemed to love it and didn't seem bored, even though it was Lipstick they came to see and not us.

The chair routine was going great and we were almost done. We were counting silently, *one, two, and three.* On the fourth and fifth count, we jumped over the chair, and on the sixth count, we landed standing up on the chair.

However, instead of landing on the chair on the sixth count, I fell on the floor and the leg of the chair completely broke off. I hit the floor on the sixth count and was up on the seventh count joining back in the routine.

She looked over at me, frowned up her face, and continued dancing like nothing ever happened. I knew everyone saw the obvious fall, and I couldn't play it off.

"I want to leave," I mumbled to Mia on stage.

"Keep dancing," she told me.

Finally, the chair routine was over and I couldn't wait to get off the stage. Once we were back in our dressing room, I started talking about how I fell. We were both laughing so hard that we couldn't stand up.

"I have never fallen on stage before. How in the hell did the leg of my chair break?" I asked Mia, while still laughing.

"Accidents happen. Don't worry about it. Were you really going to leave the stage?"

"No. I was talking out of embarrassment. I'm a professional and would never do that," I assured her.

"Good, because that would have been horrible if you would have left me on the stage alone," Mia said.

I looked at Mia and saw a satisfying look on her face. I started feeling like she was happy I had fallen. I couldn't understand how the leg of the chair broke off; I only weighed 120 pounds. I think she set me up to fail. I stared at Mia trying to figure her out.

Before I could ask her about the chair, some of our friends came to our dressing room to see us. Mia's friends told her the show would have been perfect if I hadn't fallen off the chair. My friends told me even though I fell, the show still was good.

For the rest of the night, Mia started acting like she was annoyed with me. She expressed that my fall on stage messed up her choreography. As a choreographer, I knew how it felt when a dancer makes a mistake. You feel like your entire routine is ruined. Still, she needed to get over it because I was the one that fell on my butt in front of a crowd.

After the Lipstick show, Mia and I were getting hired together all the time. We really were breaking through the industry as planned. I let the chair incident go since I didn't have any proof that she had something to do with it, but my instinct told me something different.

According to me and Mia, dark-skinned dancers were popular. The only time it got challenging was when they only wanted to hire one of us, and most of the time, I was their choice.

Mia started getting frustrated and didn't understand why they were not hiring her. Before she started dancing with me, she had no problem getting lead parts. Soon, she became very distant with me and started backing away.

~~~~~~~

"Why didn't you come to the Rhapsody audition yesterday with Mia?" one of my friends asked while we worked out at the gym.
~~~~~~~

"Mia didn't tell me about it," I said, trying not to sound alarmed.

"Girl, you should have been there. They were paying five hundred dollars for the show."

"Did you get hired?"

"Yes, and they hired three other dancers, but they didn't hire Mia."

"I hate I missed the audition."

"I thought you stopped dancing, because I've been seeing Mia at several auditions without you. Are you guys still dancing together?"

"Yes. I've been busy lately," I said, trying to hold back my anger.

"I'll call when I hear about another audition."

"Thanks."

I couldn't believe Mia was going to auditions without me. It was her idea for us to go together in the first place. As soon as I was done working out, I was going to call her.

"Mia, why are you going to auditions without me?" I asked as soon as she picked up the telephone.

"What?"

I caught her off guard with my question.

"I thought we were going to go to auditions together. I see you've been going without me," I said, irritated.

"A lot of the auditions were at the last minute and I didn't think you could make it," Mia replied.

"I thought we were working together," I said.

"We're partners," Mia said.

"Cool. I'm glad nothing has changed," I responded, giving her the same bullshit she gave me.

When I hung up, I knew that would be the last time I spoke with her. It was something in her tone that was different, and I didn't want to stick around to see what was going on with her.

I needed to stay focused and keep moving on. Besides, she was only my temporary partner. I couldn't wait for Raven to come back.

A few weeks after talking to Mia, I ran into a mutual friend of ours and I started telling him about the situation with Mia.

"Mia stopped telling you about auditions because she was tired of not getting hired for the lead parts," my friend stated.

"Now I'm her competition," I said.

He explained that if Mia continued going to auditions with me, she would never get the job she wanted.

"No one is going to bring their competition to the same audition with them. It's nothing personal, just business."

"Mia could have just told me."

"I'm going to tell you something, and you better not say anything," he said.

"Don't worry; I'm very good at keeping my mouth closed."

"Mia sabotaged your chair the night you fell. She didn't want you to shine because the singer Toss was in the audience looking for dancers, and Mia knew this. She didn't want you to get the job."

"How do you know that?"

"She's telling everyone around town about loosening the screws in your chair. She's laughing at you."

I was heated. "I'm going to beat her ass."

"It's not worth it. It's over, and you're not that type of person. Mia is jealous of you. She will never make it as a dancer because she's too busy trying to destroy everyone's career. Keep dancing and forget about her. Your revenge will be her seeing you become successful."

"I can't believe this."

"Believe it and get used to it, because this is the business that you're in. People will do anything to make it, so watch your back."

It's sad that dancers can't be friends if they want to succeed. The entertainment business divided and conquered people. I'm starting to feel like I can't have real friends in this business.

It was a lonely industry, but from now on, I decided I would dance solo until Raven came back. At least I could trust her.

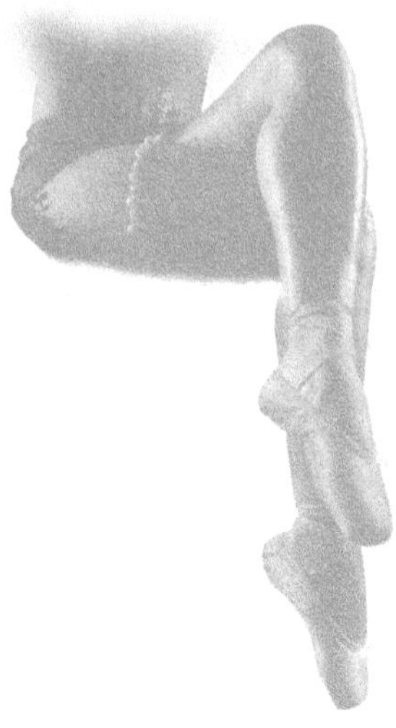

CHAPTER 8

There were few auditions and things were very slow. This was the time that I suffered the most. I wanted to dance and waiting for a gig made me restless. Even the established recording artist, could not afford to take dancers on the road.

New artists were looking for dancers, but did not have enough money to pay or they performed at horrible places, such as a lounge full of old people. Therefore, I had to be selective regarding who I worked with.

Having developed a reputation for being a great choreographer and dancer, I enjoyed creating routines as well as developing show concepts. So, I took a break from dancing and made choreography my main focus, working with almost every local artist in town.

Most people didn't understand why I chose to work with artists who were not paying or were not very popular. The reason I worked with them was to practice my craft and be prepared for whenever a platinum-selling artist wanted to hire me. It was my way of staying ahead of the game.

When I signed up to choreograph a show, I would select dancers who loved to perform and were hard workers. It was my goal to help people, even the ones who could barely keep up with an eight count. I enjoyed teaching people and watching them grow into amazing dancers.

I realized how hard it was for women of color to get jobs. So, since I was in charge of hiring dancers, I always hired a majority of dark-skinned dancers. It may have seemed like I was now the one discriminating, but of course, I hired light-skinned dancers, too. I just wanted to make sure everyone was getting jobs equally and fairly.

The dancers I hired knew they had to work hard and couldn't miss rehearsal. I demanded perfection and didn't accept any slackers. This was annoying to some because everyone wasn't in love with dancing as much as I was.

One of the hardest things about being a dancer was the cliques, which always seemed to form and make others who were not a part of them feel uncomfortable. I hated cliques because I believed in treating everyone with respect.

The business was cut throat, so I needed to watch my back at all times. If you weren't a part of a clique, no one knew you existed.

I was definitely going to change that, because I stood alone and refused to be a part of any stuck-up gossiping group. If you were cool with me, I was cool with you. It was that simple.

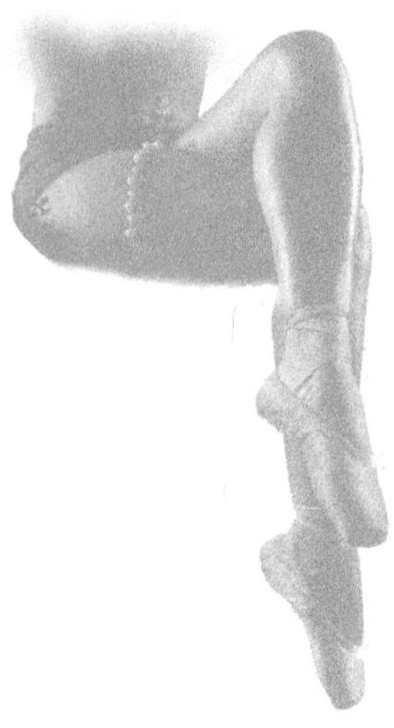

CHAPTER 9

Things had started picking up, and it was beginning to be a good year for me. There were plenty of dance jobs available, and I was working every weekend without Raven, who was becoming very popular in the modeling industry.

Raven was flying back and forth to New York doing photo shoots and hair shows. Since we hadn't danced together in over six months, I was getting use to dancing solo.

I was hired to work with a new artist named Lollipop, but we called her Lola. She was signed to a major record label, and her song was being played on every radio station. Lola hired me to work with her as a dancer and choreographer for a two-month tour.

Her manager had seen my work and personally contacted me to choreograph her entire show. He wanted me to create something that was different from anything I had ever done.

Her show had to be unique, which was my specialty. He told me to hire three more dancers that could pick up on my unique routine and show concepts, and who danced as well as I did.

Although I was no longer talking to Mia, I still remembered what she taught me and I immediately discussed pay with him. I was paid to dance, rehearsals, and for my choreography.

I needed to hire someone who knew my style of choreography and was a quick learner. So, I immediately called Raven because I knew she was back in town.

"I'm glad you answered your telephone," I said.

"You know I will always answer your call," Raven said.

"You've been a busy lady, and I'm glad you're home because I have a job for you. I hope you're available."

"I'm available. I don't have anything scheduled for the next few months."

"I was starting to think you wanted to stop dancing."

"I love dancing, but modeling is good to me right now, and I'm going to ride it until I can't ride it no more. I can always go back to dancing. Besides, the modeling world caters to me much more than the dancing world. I like getting pampered," Raven said, smacking her lips.

"Let's get you back dancing so the dynamic duo can return."

I gave Raven all the details for Lola's two-month tour. She seemed excited to be working with me again. I was also happy because I missed hanging out with my best friend. It would be like old times.

"I'm putting together a very different show for Lola. She wants something unique."

"I'm ready. I know your style well," Raven said with confidence.

"That's why I called you," I replied. "So, get ready for a lot of rehearsals."

Raven knew how I liked my shows, and it was never a problem with her practicing all the time. This show needed extra rehearsals because it was going to be very unique and whimsical.

After I hired two more dancers, we started preparing for the show. Rehearsals were going well, and Lola loved the show concepts. Raven and I had a blast talking and laughing and we was happy to be back together again.

After two weeks of rehearsing nonstop, Lola's tour started, with the first stop being in New Orleans. Raven and I cringed from our drunken memories on Bourbon Street.

The tour was successful, and Lola received a lot of compliments on her show. So far, we were all getting along and having a great time.

Working as the choreographer for the tour, I was in charge of hiring dancers and informing them about rehearsals, show dates, and any changes. For some reason, Raven started acting odd when she was given information about the tour from me. She seemed to get frustrated often.

She didn't like that I was talking directly to Lola, and had some authority over her. I didn't know why Raven had a problem with it now because it had always been that way when we worked together.

Everything had been running smoothly until Raven started to spoil the mood.

"You seem irritated with me lately," I said.

"I don't know why Lola doesn't tell me what's going on with the show or tour information," she sneered.

"Raven, you know how it works. They tell me and I tell you guys. Nothing has changed. Everything still works the same," I told her.

"Things need to change," Raven replied.

"Where is this coming from? What's up with you?" I said with frustration.

Ever since Raven started modeling, she was a different person. I noticed she didn't want people telling her what to do. She wanted to be in charge and run the show.

Going behind my back, Raven started talking to Lola about the show during the tour and couldn't wait to tell me about the information she had received. I didn't understand why it was a big deal how she found out, but to her, it seemed very important.

"Lola wants us to meet in the lobby an hour early today for sound check," Raven informed me and the other dancers. "See, Music, you're not the only one to find out information."

“What are you talking about?” I asked, frowning.

“I will speak directly to Lola from now on. I don’t need you to pass on information to me,” she said.

I just looked at Raven and shook my head. She was truly acting crazy. This was not necessary. The other dancers shook their heads too, and walked out of the room.

“Don’t get mad because you’re not the only one in charge,” Raven said.

“This has nothing to do with authority, Raven. I just want us to dance together with no drama. But, you’re on another page.”

My comments didn’t seem to faze her. She smiled while getting ready for sound check. It was important for her to have a connection with the artist. I knew it happened with other dancers, but I didn’t think it would be an issue with her. It was obvious she wanted my spot.

In the middle of the tour, Raven came up with some ideas and wanted to make changes to the show. She even wanted to create some dance moves. I was in total shock because Raven was never into choreographing.

“Why didn’t you show me your choreography during rehearsals?” I asked her.

“I don’t have to show you anything,” Raven said nastily.

She kept insisting that Lola take a look at some of the changes she made. Lola didn’t mind looking at the steps, but she didn’t want to change the show in the middle of her tour. When Lola overheard us talking one day, she came to me wanting to know what was up with Raven.

“What’s going on with your girl?” Lola asked me.

“I’m not sure,” I replied.

“Can you talk to her? I don’t want to change my show in the middle of the tour. Handle that situation,” she said.

“I will take care of it.”

“Thanks, Music. I don’t need any distractions on the road.”

I really didn't want to talk to her because I knew it wouldn't make a difference, but I had to do my job. As I promised Lola, I tried talking with Raven before our show.

"Maybe you can show me some of your choreography after the tour," I told her, trying to make peace.

"Why can't you look at it now?"

"We are about to go on stage in an hour. We don't have time," I replied.

"Are you jealous of me?" Raven asked.

"Jealous! Ever since you started modeling you have been acting stupid."

"Music, you just don't want me to get close to Lola because you're scared I might take your job. You're scared they might like my choreography better than yours."

"You're not the same person. What is wrong with you?" I asked, totally irritated.

"There's nothing wrong with me. I'm Raven, and I have not changed. I'm still the same fierce, fabulous bitch, and you can't handle it."

"You're fierce, but your attitude is fucked up and far from fabulous. Remember, I'm the one who called and hired you for this job. If I were jealous of you, why would I have called you?"

"You called me because I'm the best dancer you know."

"There's a way to handle everything," I responded. "You're not being professional right now. Who in the hell changes their show in the middle of a tour because a dancer has an idea?"

I walked out of our dressing room and slammed the door before she could say a word. I was very furious and had to calm down.

The rest of the tour was awkward because Raven wouldn't talk to me, and I wasn't trying to talk to her either. She became very quiet and distant. I don't know what happened to her when she went to New York to pursue her modeling career, but this wasn't my best friend.

Raven had really changed, and her rollercoaster behavior was becoming tiring. Sure, we all wanted the spotlight, but I didn't flip out on my friends to get it. I understand now that I can't have friends in this business.

After the tour, we didn't talk much. She would text me once in a while to make small talk, but I couldn't keep talking or working with her knowing that she was treating me differently.

She had been rude and disrespectful, and now that I knew exactly how she felt about me, she needed to get her own dance jobs because I would no longer be helping her.

The pampering she received from the modeling industry has messed with her ego. She was out of control and thought everything revolved around her.

I didn't know her anymore and needed a break from her and her big ego. Years of friendship down the drain. Damn this business.

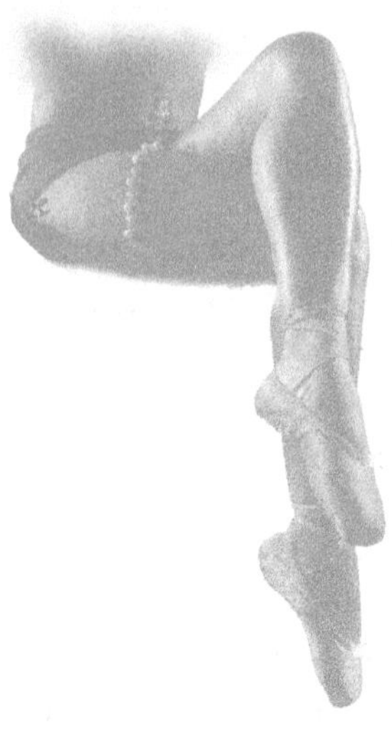

CHAPTER 10

Months passed and I continued focusing on creating elaborate shows for local artist. I also continued to stay distant from Raven, which was a good break for me. I didn't call her for auditions. Instead, I let her concentrate on pursuing her modeling career.

I started working with a new recording artist called Rocky, who kept me busy with shows every weekend. He sang about love, and his songs were beautiful. He was a great person and singer. He delivered the songs in a very romantic presentation on stage. His talents were impressive.

I created an intricate show for him that was a hit every time. The only problem was the locations where Rocky performed. He did the club and lounge appearances like every new artist, and no one important ever saw his show.

I was happy to only be choreographing his shows, because I didn't want to dance at the type of places he was performing at. Dancing for people at lounges was not fun, because they were always too drunk or just didn't pay attention to the performance.

Rocky was selected to perform at a music showcase, which was a huge event that just about every entertainer in the business was attending. Every new artist prepared for this showcase.

Rocky was hoping to get a record deal, and he worked extra hard to make sure his show was a hit. Even though we had only one month to prepare, I was determined to choreograph something different and exceptional. I hired two dancers and worked them night and day to create a great show.

I met with a popular designer to rent a signature design from his collection for the dancers. While most dancers were half naked, they were going to be dressed in black suits, matching Dobb hats, and wing-tip shoes.

Rocky knew he was taking a risk being so different with his show concept, but he was willing to trust my instincts. I felt confident that this was the way we should go with his show. I convinced him that a different show would make him stand out, and therefore, he agreed to try something different.

He was willing to give my creativity a try. This was a chance for important people in the music industry to hear him sing, and I wanted him to get good reviews.

After long hours of rehearsing, we finally got the show where we wanted it. The dancers worked the stage and complemented Rocky, while looking beautiful and classy in their suits. Rocky and his manager, Frank, were very pleased with my work, and he felt ready to take over the seminar.

Three days before the showcase, one of the dancers sprained her ankle and couldn't perform at the show. Nicole was extremely upset because she was afraid she wouldn't be able to perform since her partner was injured.

Naturally, everyone panicked. I tried to get another dancer to replace her on short notice, but had no luck. I even went back on my word and tried to contact Raven to see if she was available, but she had a fashion show scheduled the same day of the showcase.

Rocky was mad because of all the hard work he had put into the rehearsals. He wanted to cancel the show, but Frank refused to let him throw all his efforts down the drain.

"The show will go on with or without dancers," Frank said.

Rocky was upset about Frank's decision because he loved what the dancers added to his show.

"Music, I need you to fill in for this show," Rocky said desperately.

“I don’t want to dance,” I told him.

“I really want to use dancers, and you’re the only one that knows the routine. Please,” he pleaded.

I really was comfortable with not dancing, but I didn’t want his show to suffer. Wanting my creativity to be seen, I agreed to dance. They were excited and couldn’t stop thanking me.

“We’re going to have to rehearse a little more so I can get my place on stage and get comfortable with Nicole,” I told them.

“Whatever you need, it’s done. Thanks for helping,” Frank said.

“No problem. Now, let’s get to work and get Rocky a record deal.”

“That’s why I love you, Music. You’re always willing to help out. You need to get serious about singing and let us help you get a record deal,” Rocky said, while giving me a hug.

“I’m not really interested in singing,” I replied.

“You have an incredible voice. It would be easy to get you a record deal,” Frank added.

“Thanks, but right now, I just want to focus on choreographing and dancing.”

People were always mesmerized when they heard me sing. Usually, I would just sing around the house, not trying to sound great. Maybe when I get tired of dancing, I will focus on singing.

I needed to tell Nicole what was going on so she could stop worrying. I decided to give her a call.

“Nicole, I’m going to fill in for the show.”

“Thank you Music!” She yelled into the phone.

“We need to rehearse a few more days so I can get familiar with everything.”

“Not more rehearsals,” Nicole said jokingly.

“I only need a day or two,” I told her.

"No problem. I'm excited to be dancing with you."

"Thanks, Nicole. See you at rehearsal tomorrow."

Nicole and I rehearsed the next day to make sure everything would go smoothly, and we looked great together. Rocky couldn't stop smiling because he was so happy everything was still going as planned.

Nicole was very petite, with a light caramel complexion and slanted eyes. She was half African American and half Chinese. She also spoke Chinese fluently. Her skin looked like a cup of coffee with extra cream. She was so beautiful that she should have been a model.

Although Nicole had no formal training and wasn't a great dancer, but she loved to dance. Therefore, I was willing to take extra time to help her. It was challenging because I had to break down every dance step. The reason why I hired Nicole for shows in the past was because she had that extra spark I liked.

At first, she was stiff and awkward, but after working with her one-on-one, she got the dance routines. It took a lot of time and I was frustrated teaching her, because she was very slow at learning. She didn't want to rehearse all the time, but frankly she needed to.

"How much longer do we have to rehearse today?" Nicole asked.

"Not long," I said.

Rocky made a change in the show, so I had to revise it. This meant working with Nicole longer than expected.

"Music, you're the only person I know who truly loves dancing and rehearsing," Nicole said, laughing.

"I love what I do, and rehearsing makes things perfect," I responded.

"Thanks for working with me. I know it's been a struggle for you," Nicole said.

"No problem. I enjoy helping you. As long as you want to work hard, I'm willing to help you. Rehearsing is the only way you're going to get better. If you want to make it in this business, you need to be excellent."

“I’m very excited about this show. There are going to be a lot of famous people there. I’m trying to meet my future husband,” Nicole said, as we both laughed and gave each other high-fives.

“Well, I was told it’s going to be fun and a lot of good looking men will be there,” I said, while smiling and rubbing my hands together.

“I hope you don’t run into your ex-boyfriend,” Nicole said.

“Yuck!” I replied.

My ex-boyfriend, Doug, worked in the entertainment industry and was always at music events. I was not looking forward to running into him since I didn’t have too much to say to a cheater.

“With all the fine men there, you won’t be thinking about him.”

“My personal life is fine right now. I’m dating and met a guy I really like,” I told her.

I had to learn quickly that being a dancer in this industry meant my personal life would suffer. It was hard for men to understand not seeing their girlfriend all the time. Sometimes I got tired of explaining why I couldn’t hang out for the night because I had rehearsal for a show.

I wanted a serious relationship but it seemed like it wasn’t going to happen. I was hopeful for the new guy I was seeing, but if it didn’t work out again because of my career, I would mend my heart and keep working. Right now, dancing is more important to me than a relationship.

“I saw your new guy and he’s cute,” Nicole said.

“He is handsome, but I’m taking it slow. I’ll see how things go because most good-looking men are cheaters.”

“I know what you mean. Men ain’t shit.”

“Stop all the men bashing and finish rehearsing so we can get out of here,” Rocky said, as he entered the room.

“Good, because we have been rehearsing too long,” Nicole replied.

I looked at her, shook my head, and laughed. I couldn’t understand a person that needed to rehearse, but never wanted to.

It was the day of the showcase, and we were ready but anxious. The showcase was held at a huge convention center, and it looked like everyone in town was attending.

Those who were interested in working in the music and getting a record deal attended the showcase. There were entertainers, songwriters, music moguls, and record executives attending the event.

Of course, the lobby was filled with people trying to get a glimpse of their favorite entertainers. Some entertainers walked around like normal people, while other entertainers had a huge entourage with security that made them untouchable to the public.

It was crowded in the lobby, but we managed to push our way through to make it to our dressing room. There were several thousand people attending, and everyone was waiting for the new talent showcase, which was the last event of the day.

The performers were going to be critiqued by a celebrity panel. This wasn't a showcase where a winner was selected. It was a showcase where you would have your music reviewed and get professional advice from veterans in the industry.

Everyone who performed met one-on-one with the celebrities to discuss their career. We worked hard to make sure his show would be incredible, and we were ready.

Nicole and I peeked in the ballroom before the show and could see the room was packed with celebrity judges sitting directly in front of the stage.

"I have butterflies in my stomach," Nicole said.

"I'm used to dancing in front of crowds, but not in front of so many celebrities," I responded, as butterflies also started forming in my stomach.

"I can't believe how many people are here," Nicole commented.

"I'm nervous knowing that they're going to critique our show," I expressed.

"I hope I don't mess up the routine," she said.

"You will be fine. Just pretend you're at rehearsal and work that stage."

We both took a deep breath and started stretching. We said a prayer and hit the stage like professionals. Rocky sang his heart out, while the crowd cheered and screamed.

The reception from the audience made Nicole and I feel like a million bucks and we didn't want the show to end. The hardest part was waiting for the celebrity panel to critique our performance. The producers on the panel gave Rocky good advice and told him they loved his songs.

One of the celebrity recording artists said, "I loved the show, the choreography, the dancers and the outfits."

I was on cloud nine. It was nice to hear people in the business confirming to me that what I created was amazing. It made me feel like I could choreograph a show for a major artist.

Another artist said, "Your stage show was very good, but you should work on the tone of your voice. I loved the show, but I didn't like the music."

Rocky took a deep breath and tried to stay humble while listening to the critiques about his singing.

"I really loved the show, and if I could steal your dancers, I would take them with me today," Slyy, the celebrity artist said.

His comment made me so happy that I wanted to scream on stage, but I remained poised and quietly replied, "Thank you."

Slyy was a multi-platinum selling singer and had won several Grammys. He started off as an actor and then started singing. He had won an Oscar and was an incredible actor.

His fans were disappointed when he decided to stop acting and completely focus on singing. He enjoyed acting and promised his fans he would return someday.

Nicole and I left the stage mesmerized, while Rocky was happy but a little bummed by the bad critiques.

"He wanted to take us with him," Nicole said excitedly.

"I wonder if he really meant what he said," I told her.

I didn't believe Slyy and figured he was just being nice with the Hollywood talk, which was usually a bunch of nonsense.

"Let's get dressed and find him to see if he's serious," I said, determined to confront him about his comment.

We headed to our dressing room to change our clothes and then search for Slyy. On the way to our dressing room, we ran right into Slyy and his entourage.

Remembering who we were, he said, "You're the dancers from the show."

"Yes," Nicole and I replied.

"Who choreographed the show?" Slyy quickly asked.

"I did, and I also created the show concepts," I replied.

"You did an awesome job. What's your name?"

"Music," I said, thrilled.

"What a cool name. It's nice to meet you, Music. You did a great job," Slyy said, while shaking my hand.

"Thank you. This is Nicole," I said, introducing them.

"Are you girls interested in going on tour with me?" he asked us.

"Yes! When are we leaving?" I asked eagerly.

Rocky's manager, Frank, walked up while we were talking and interrupted us by introducing himself. He joined in our conversation telling Slyy how great we were. He sounded like he was our manager.

"We love working with these girls. Here's Rocky's album. Listen to it and let me know what you think. Maybe we can work together some day," Frank said.

However, Slyy didn't seem interested in Rocky's album. "Give the CD to my assistant. I'm more interested in hiring these girls for my tour," he bluntly told Frank.

"That's great! I can hook that up for you," Frank told him.

Nicole and I looked at Frank trying to make a deal for us and were a little annoyed that he wasn't letting us handle it ourselves. We were stunned by what was going on, but not saying a word, we let Frank handle the deal.

"Give my assistant Garret your number, and he'll be in touch with you tomorrow regarding the details for the girls," Slyy said.

"No problem. I'll be waiting for the call," Frank told him, then handed Garrett his business card.

"I'll see you girls soon," Slyy said, as he walked away before we could say anything to him.

The next day, I got a call from Frank, who said Slyy wanted me to choreograph a routine for one of the songs on his new album. He also wanted us to be ready for a show in one week.

I asked him if Slyy would get a chance to see the routine. Frank replied by saying that after seeing the show I put together, Slyy said he trusted I would hook his show up. He told me to keep it in line with the show I put together for Rocky. I started feeling the pressure and still could not believe it was happening so fast.

Surprisingly, Slyy was being true to his word. I was so excited that I started making calls to tell all my friends and family.

"Mom, Guess what?" I said excitedly.

"What's going on?" My mother asked.

"I got hired to dance for Slyy on his tour!" I yelled in the telephone.

"Who?" She asked, sounding extremely shocked.

"Slyy, the Grammy winning singer!" I said ecstatic.

My mother didn't say anything.

"Did you hear me, Mom? I'm going on tour with Slyy. This is my dream. I've finally made it!"

Still, my mom didn't say a word.

"Hello. Are you there, Mom?"

"I don't think that's a good idea," she finally said.

"Why?" I asked.

"Because you know how wild and crazy those entertainers are."

"Mom, this is my dream. Can you at least be happy for me?"

"Music, I don't want you to go on tour with Slyy. I want you to finish college. You have a job. Why can't you be happy with that?"

"Why can't you be happy for me? I don't know why I called you. You never supported me, but I thought this time you would be excited." I snapped.

"I don't want you to go on tour with Slyy."

"I'm a grown woman, and I'm going on tour."

"Music, you're not ready for life on the road."

"How do you know? You've never been on tour, and you don't know what life on the road is like."

"You shouldn't go," she simply replied.

"I don't want to talk about this anymore. I'm going rather you like it or not. Thanks for being so supportive, Mom," I said sarcastically, than hung up without saying goodbye.

~~~~~~~

Nicole and I practiced every day. I was not going to screw up this opportunity. We only had one week to prepare, and once again, Nicole was getting tired of rehearsing.

"Nicole, we have to work extra hard," I told her.

"We need to take a break," she responded.

"We don't have time to take a break. I need to make sure you know the routines. You know it takes you a long time to catch on," I said, really frustrated.

"I'll get it."
~~~~~~~

"Let's stay focused and keep practicing."

"I'm tired of rehearsing," Nicole said worn out.

"We are going into a different territory. We have to be ready. Slyy is taking a chance on us, and we need to deliver."

"You're a workaholic."

"We're dancing for Slyy!" I emphasized, while jumping up and down.

With all the rehearsing and preparation to leave in a week, we hadn't let it sink in.

"I'm so excited. We made it!" Nicole shouted.

I wanted to make sure we were on point, so I forced her to continue rehearsing everyday as long as we needed to. I wanted Slyy to love the routine, and I definitely didn't want him to regret hiring us.

Even though we never discussed how much we were getting paid for the show or my choreography, it didn't matter to me because I was too thrilled to be working with Slyy.

I had no worries because my dreams were becoming a reality. It was what I'd been waiting for, and I wasn't going to let anyone take it away from me.

If Raven wasn't acting so crazy, she would have been here to experience it with me. It had been months since we had spoken to each other in person. We only communicated through text messages once in a while just to say a quick hello.

The next day Slyy's manager contacted me and informed me of our salary. We were getting paid $1200 per week and $250 Per Diem for our weekly food allowance.

I was so excited that I almost dropped the telephone. I tried to pretend like I was accustomed to getting paid this amount.

"You will sign all the paperwork at the first show," his manager said.

I couldn't dial Nicole's number fast enough to tell her how much we were getting paid. Nicole screamed when I told her the amount.

"We're rich!" We both yelled.

~~~~~~~

Three days passed and Rocky's manager, Frank called to tell me that we were getting our airline tickets in the mail the next day.

Slyy wanted us to wear the same outfits we wore for the showcase. He loved the show concept I created and wanted to use it for his new tour. The suits and hats was how he envisioned his show concept to be.

I immediately contacted the designer that we got the suits from. He was more than willing to give us the suits once he heard they would be used for Slyy's tour. He even gave Slyy a discounted rate and requested to have his name printed in the tour book as the designer, and Slyy agreed.

Frank also mentioned that Slyy's assistant, Garrett, would be calling me to discuss the details of the tour. Two hours later, I received the call.

"Hello, is this Music?"

"Yes. Who is this?"

"This is Garrett, Slyy's assistant. You should have been expecting my call."

"Yes, I was."

"Well, get a pen and paper ready. Time is money, and I don't have enough of either," Garrett said with a major attitude.

He discussed how we would get paid and he gave me part of the tour schedule. Slyy had a few shows to do before the tour, and Garrett was very adamant about us proving our skills during those shows.

"I will see you next week," he said.

Before I could say goodbye, Garrett hung up.

I shook off the feeling of wanting to strangle him through the telephone, and called my job to request time off for next week, using all my saved vacation time.
~~~~~~~

The next day, Frank called and told me to make sure I gave Rocky's CD to Slyy again. I agreed and told him that I would make sure he got it. I knew Frank wanted me to hook them up, especially since we had gotten a job.

I couldn't make Slyy give Rocky a record deal, but I could make sure he got his music. I felt bad that we had gotten a chance to work with Slyy, while Rocky didn't. I almost felt guilty.

When everyone heard I got hired to work with Slyy, they expected me to hook them up with a job. They didn't understand that I hadn't gotten in the door good enough to help anyone but myself.

Every dancer I knew was calling and dropping off their headshot and resume. Even Mia stopped by to give me her information. I hadn't spoken with her in a long time, so I couldn't believe she had the audacity to stop by my house.

The same dancers who never told me about any auditions wanted me to hook them up. It was very stressful, and I was ready to leave to avoid talking to anyone else.

I only felt obligated to hook Rocky up. If it wasn't for us dancing in his show, we would have never met Slyy. Nicole and I owed him, so I would try to help him as much as I could.

CHAPTER 11

A week later, Nicole and I were on an airplane headed to New York City to perform on a television show with Slyy. I still couldn't understand why Slyy didn't want to see the routine in advance.

Once we landed, Slyy's limo picked us up from the airport and took us straight to sound check. We were already getting first-class service. We were terrified and didn't know what to expect.

At sound check, we were going to run through the entire show. While we rehearsed on stage, the crew would make sure Slyy sounded great in his microphone and the lights were set up properly.

When the limo pulled up to the backstage door, Garrett was standing there waiting impatiently. I remembered how he looked from meeting him at the showcase.

He was much older than Slyy, but in great shape. He was bald, with big, beautiful light brown eyes, and a well-groomed beard. He was dressed impeccably, wearing an Armani suit with Versace cufflinks. His Gucci shoes matched his suit perfectly, and the Louis Vuitton ascot around his neck completed his look.

His nails were well groomed and he smelled wonderful. His teeth were white as paper, and his skin looked like silk butter. He spoke in a low, relaxed tone, but with much authority in his voice. You knew he was not one to play with.

"Hello, Music and Nicole," Garrett greeted us.

"Hey," We both said.

"Hay is for horses. Please say hello," Garrett snapped at us.

"Hello," Nicole and I replied, embarrassed.

"Hurry up because we're about to start sound check and you guys need to run through the routine."

After entering the building, we started walking down a long hallway. Some of the crew took our bags and put them in our dressing room. As Garrett was talking fast and giving us the itinerary for the day, we tried to keep up with him.

This was different from any of my other dance jobs because you could smell money and power in the air. Garrett walked and talked, giving us the time of the sound check, the time the show started, what time we needed to be ready, and what the itinerary would be for the next few days.

We were looking around at all the stars pictures on the wall. Noticing that we were falling behind, Garrett told us to keep up and handed us a sheet of paper with everything on it he had just explained. I was glad it was written down, because with all the excitement, I knew I wouldn't remember anything he said.

It was still sinking in that we were on the set of a famous television show in New York City. I was overwhelmed and looking around like a tourist. This was really big for us, but we were trying to act like it didn't faze us. Even though we wanted to go running down the hallway screaming, flipping, and yelling from excitement, we kept our composure.

"Pay attention and listen closely. Slyy hired you guys and he can fire you, too. So, don't screw this up. You got a great opportunity, so take it seriously. We are professionals here," Garrett said.

We looked at each other wondering what else he was going to say next.

Garrett continued speaking. "Here are the rules of the road, and don't forget them because I'm only going to tell you once."

We were now listening closely.

"Act like an adult at all times. You must always look beautiful and sexy. No exceptions! You must always wear heels and makeup. You must keep your hair done, dress fashionably, and keep your body in shape. There are gyms at every hotel we stay at. So, there is no excuse for fat on your body."

We looked at each other like we had just signed up for the army. He was killing our mood.

"Keep your nails perfectly manicured. No fake nails or bright nail polish allowed. That's just tacky. Always be on time for sound check, shows and anything else Slyy wants you to attend. I assume you guys can dance, because I know Slyy would not have hired you if you couldn't." He said looking us up and down like he didn't approve.

Garrett paused to take a deep breath and then continued.

"No one has seen you dance before. So, for your sake, you better work that stage. When I speak, you listen and do what I say. I don't like repeating myself. If you have questions, ask me."

Nicole and I kept staring at each other. Garrett was like a drill sergeant, and it seemed like he would never shut up.

"Everything on this tour is confidential. You're not to repeat anything to anyone about what is happening on the road. If you do, you will be fired, sued, or worse," he said seriously.

"What do you mean by that?" Nicole asked.

Garrett quickly looked at her and bucked his eyes. "You better be able to keep secrets. The road is full of them, and we don't need people who talk too much. If you want to make it in this business, keep your damn mouth shut. Do we have an understanding?"

"Yes, we understand," Nicole and I replied.

All that information took the thrill from us, and we started to see how serious this was going to be.

When we walked into sound check, the band was playing, Slyy was on stage singing with a girl dancing around him, and the crew was checking the sound equipment.

"You're going to be performing as soon as Slyy finishes this song," Garrett informed us.

It was all happening too soon, and I needed more time. Although we were trying not to act like big fans, the truth is we were huge fans and wanted to run on stage and tear Slyy's clothes off.

My insides were jittery and my heart was pounding fast. I was finally living my dream. I closed my eyes for a second and said a quick prayer.

I knew when the music started all eyes were going to be on us, which was terrifying since I had never performed with a live band before. The band sounded great, much better than the song on the album.

Nicole and I watched Slyy's every move. As the girl danced around him like a professional. I knew I had to shake off my nerves to avoid looking scared. I deserved to be here and I was going to give it all I had.

Garrett took us to the side of the stage and told us to get ready. I had so many questions, but didn't want to look like I didn't know what I was doing. Not to mention, Garrett's appearance and demeanor were intimidating.

"When do we go on stage?" I asked him.

Garrett looked at me like I was crazy. He opened his eyes wide, stared at me for a few seconds, and then said very sarcastically, "You're the dancer. Figure it out. You should know what to do."

"Okay," I replied.

I didn't want to start off looking inexperienced to him, but I knew he could tell I was. My lack of experience dancing on a large tour definitely showed. At this point, I knew I had gotten on his nerves.

Garrett continued staring at me, and walked away while mumbling to himself, "Why in the hell did Slyy hire them?" I knew then not to ask him another question.

Since we never rehearsed an entrance onto the stage, I quickly told Nicole, "When the music starts, walk on stage like a model. Act like you're walking the catwalk. Walk slowly to your position and get there before it's time to start the routine."

I knew a slow, sexy walk would work and be simple enough for Nicole to catch on to. She agreed, and we both waited for our cue to go on stage.

"Let's rock this," I said, while looking at Nicole.

She looked at me and said, "Let's do it."

When the music began playing, we walked on stage. I was on cloud nine, only hearing and feeling the drums, keyboard, and bass. I didn't see Nicole on stage because I was totally focused. In my mind, I was all alone on stage, and I was going to let the music move me.

Slyy, Garrett, and a few other people sat front and center to watch our performance. As Slyy sang the song from his seat, I hit the stage and gave it everything I had. I pretended like the place was filled with millions of people and performed like it was the actual show.

After we finished dancing, Slyy spoke in the microphone and said, "Music, let me talk to you."

I wasn't sure what was going on, but I hoped it was good news.

As Nicole waited on stage, I walked down the stairs and out into the empty seats, while trying not to look worried. Slyy signaled for the band to continue to play.

"Hello Music. I'm glad you guys made it. You look good on stage," Slyy said.

"Thanks. I'm happy to be here."

"This is my dancer Blanca. She's been with me for a couple of months, and now she will have to share the stage," Slyy said, as he winked at her.

He also introduced me to his girlfriend Janice, his security guards, and a few record executives. This was starting to feel like a dream.

"It's nice to meet you, Music. I loved your choreography and performance," Janice said.

"Thank you," I replied, amazed.

"I thought Nicole was on the same level as you are when it came to dancing," Slyy said.

"She knows the routine. She's just nervous," I told him.

"She didn't look that horrible when I met you guys in Chicago," Slyy added, confused.

He didn't know that we had a month to prepare for Rockys' show versus one week to prepare for his show.

"You need to work with Nicole because I'm not happy with her performance. She's stiff and looks awful," Janice said firmly. "If she doesn't get the routine, she has to go home."

My heart dropped when I heard that. I needed to work with Nicole and pray that she would get better in a couple of hours before the show.

Once I got a good look at Slyy's girlfriend, I knew she was the famous actress I'd seen many times in movies and magazines. I couldn't believe I was talking to the legendary singer Slyy and his famous girlfriend Janice.

They met when Slyy was doing a movie and they instantly fell in love. They were Hollywood's hottest couple. Janice, who was an incredible actress and very beautiful, had done numerous major movies and won an Oscar.

It took everything in me to listen to what they were saying because my insides were too busy jumping up and down from excitement.

Janice continued telling me how unhappy she was with Nicole's performance. "She can't dance, and we're not going to be wasting money on her. She can be replaced."

I gasped for air from her comment.

"She acted like she was confused the whole time she performed, and she's not sexy," Janice stated.

"I'll work with her. I'm sure she was just scared," I explained.

Why didn't they tell Nicole about how horrible her performance was instead of making it my duty? I thought to myself. Maybe they didn't want to hurt her feelings, so I wasn't going to hurt her feeling either.

I walked back on stage to Nicole, who was waiting eagerly.

"What did he say?" Nicole immediately asked.

"He introduced me to his entourage and told me about the show concept."

"Did they like our performance?"

I lied and said, "Yes, but we need to work on it more."

She seemed pleased with the information. I really couldn't hurt her feelings, although I wish they would have just told her themselves. I didn't want to do their dirty work.

"They want us to rehearse before the show, so let's get started," I told Nicole.

This time while we were on stage, I watched Nicole to see what she was doing wrong, and she looked pitiful. I didn't know what was going on with her. She didn't look like that when we were rehearsing at home. I look like she was just nervous and needed to get the jitterbugs out.

Rehearsal seemed to be going well, and I was happy she could get through the routines without messing up. After we finished rehearsing, we went to the dressing room, which was nice and comfortable. Blanca was already in the room putting on her makeup.

Nicole and I immediately went to the table of food and loaded our plates with baked chicken, mashed potatoes, string beans, and chocolate cake. Nicole opened a can of soda and drunk it straight down.

Blanca looked at our plates of food and rolled her eyes. She was not use to dancers eating such a heavy meal before a show, and she definitely would not have been eating the mashed potatoes.

"You guys need to be ready in an hour, so you should start getting dressed now," Blanca said, peeved.

"Okay," we replied, while stuffing the food in our mouths.

After cleaning our plates, we went for seconds. Blanca was bothered by us. We were not acting like the dancers she knew. The truth was we were not like any dancer she knew; we were very different. I just looked at Blanca, who had a small plate of string beans in front of her and a bottle of water.

Nicole and I finished eating and started getting dressed. Blanca never said another word to us.

It was finally show time, and we were ready to go on stage to film the television show.

"Relax and everything will be fine. You know the routine, so just do it like we rehearsed," I told Nicole.

We looked at each other and hugged. All of our family and friends were watching and we wanted to make them proud.

Slyy met us on the side of the stage and said, "Let's hold hands." Then he said a quick prayer. "It's show time, girls. Show me what you got."

We clapped and headed on stage. During the show, I was not sure how Nicole did because I was focused on myself, but I hoped she was working it.

After the show, Garrett said, "The van will take you guys to the hotel. Make sure you read the itineraries I gave you. You will be riding with Blanca and the band members. If you have any questions, give me a call. My number is on the itinerary. I run a tight ship, so don't fuck it up."

Without saying a word, we quickly got in the van. We met the band members, who welcomed us to the tour. On the other hand, Blanca didn't utter a word. She just ignored us and sent text messages during the entire ride to the hotel.

We looked over the itinerary for the next ten days, and saw that we had ten shows in ten different cities: Los Angeles, Chicago, New Orleans, Texas, Virginia, Detroit, St. Louis, New Jersey, Indianapolis, and Michigan. We were not aware there were so many dates. We would be flying to all the cities starting the next day.

The other itinerary listed a nine-month tour with four months of rehearsal. *How in the world am I going to take off this much time from work?* I was stressing out, and Nicole was feeling the same way.

We were both happy, but concerned about what we were going to do about our jobs. I needed to call my job and schedule more time off. *What if this doesn't work out? I need my job.* I needed to figure this out quick.

After arriving at the posh five-star hotel, Nicole and I went our separate ways since we each had our own room. This was great because I needed time to myself to think.

Once inside my room, I immediately made calls to my friends and family to get some advice. My family felt that I shouldn't quit my job just in case the tour didn't last. Of course, my mom was telling me to come home and stop dancing, and I regretted that I call her. My friends said I should leave my job and step out on faith, since this had always been my dream.

With having to pay rent, a car note, and other monthly bills, I really needed to make the right decision. I took a long, hot bath and decided to make my decision after the ten-city tour. After bathing, I called Nicole to see what she decided to do.

"I'm going to call my job in the morning and quit," Nicole said.

"I'm going to wait and see how everything works out before I quit my job," I told her.

"Girl, this is the opportunity we've been waiting for, and I'm not going to let my job get in the way," Nicole responded, getting caught up with enjoying the star treatment.

"Maybe you should wait before you quit your job."

"I know what I'm doing."

"I'm just saying don't move so quickly," I suggested.

"Music, I'm grown, and I'm going to quit. I'm not scared."

"I'm not scared either. I'm just being smart. You should probably wait."

"Do not tell me what to do!"

"Nicole, I'm just trying to help."

"Well, I don't need your help."

"What's wrong with you?"

“I don’t like when people try to tell me what to do.”

“I’m sorry. I won’t say anything else.”

“Good!”

“I’ll talk to you later,” I said, then hung up.

~~~~~~~

The shows were going good so far, and the band members were making them enjoyable. Nicole and I never danced on stage with Blanca and hardly spent any time with her. She was very distant, and it was taking her time to warm up to us.

Blanca was very curvy, with caramel-colored skin, short blonde spiked hair, and plenty of tattoos. Whenever she performed, she covered her tattoos with makeup and wore a wig, turning into a very classy and elegant person on stage. She was from Brazil and spoke with an accent.

Blanca was a trained dancer and had been dancing all of her life. She never worked a regular nine to five job, which she was proud of. She always danced on tours or did music videos to support herself and was well-known in the entertainment industry.

She was nice, arrogant, and nasty all the time. She was used to being catered to and demanded anyone around her to do so.

“I was Slyy’s first and only dancer until he hired you guys. Slyy wanted a hip-hop flare to his show. That’s the only reason why you guys are here. He knows I don’t jump around on stage,” Blanca told us.

She made us feel like low-class, ghetto hip-hop dancers. She was one of those women you could be friends with, but you better not trust. She was used to being the number one star, the person in the spotlight, and she was not going to let anyone take that away from her.

I didn’t care about taking her spot or wanting the main spotlight. I just wanted a spot somewhere on the stage. I wanted the opportunity and of course, the pay.
~~~~~~~

So, she was worrying for the wrong reasons because we were not her competition. She couldn't compare to us because we were all very different dancers.

In between the shows, I worked with Nicole and focused on the things Slyy and Janice mentioned.

"Why are you working me so hard? You don't seem to be focusing on things you're doing wrong," Nicole said.

"I'm working just as hard as you are to make our performance better," I told her.

We had only been rehearsing a few days and she was complaining already.

"I'm tired of rehearsing and tired of you telling me what to do."

Nicole was turned on by the lifestyle of the rich and famous. Riding in limos, staying at five-star hotels, and receiving star treatment gave her a big head. She loved that part of it, but she didn't want to work on what got her all these perks.

Nicole was getting on my last nerve, complaining about rehearsing when she knew she needed it. Slyy and Janice loved my performance and I was doing this to help her out. With her attitude, I didn't know why I kept trying.

"Why do I continue to help you?" I asked Nicole.

"I don't know, but I wish you'd stop because you're driving me crazy," she responded.

I ended the rehearsal and told Nicole we would start again tomorrow. I was tired of spending all my time focusing on her, especially since she didn't want the help. So, I decided the best thing to do was tell her the truth. I waited until later that day and called her room to talk.

"Nicole, I need to talk to you."

"About what?"

"About rehearsing,"

“You want to rehearse some more? Damn,” Nicole said, irritated.

“No, I wanted to tell you why we’ve been rehearsing so much.”

I began to tell Nicole what Slyy and Janice said about her performance and that they were not happy with her. I explained that was the only reason we were rehearsing so much.

“You’re just jealous,” Nicole replied with an attitude.

“Why would I be jealous of you?” I shouted.

“If they hated my performance so much, why am I still here?”

“They are trying to give you a chance. They want me to work with you to see if you will improve.”

“I can’t believe you would make up something like this.”

“Nicole, you’re tripping right now.”

“I think I’m making you feel insecure by giving you a run for your money,” she shot back with confidence.

“Why is that the first thing a dancer thinks? You’re on your own. Let’s see how far you get now.”

“That’s good, because I’m tired of rehearsing with you!”

“Just remember I’m not going to help you anymore. Do it yourself.”

“I will.” Nicole said, than hung up.

She was on a major ego trip and needed to come back to reality. Why would she think I was jealous of her? I’m the one who showed her how to dance. I would dance circles around Nicole, and she knew it. Oh well, I wasn’t going to try to figure her out.

This wasn’t the person I knew and helped. I practically begged Slyy to let her stay and I couldn’t believe she was acting like this. Trying to stay a cool and helpful person was getting old.

~~~~~~~

We finished the ten-city tour and were about to start rehearsals for Slyy’s
~~~~~~~

world tour. Slyy and Janice were still complaining about how bad Nicole's performance was.

I didn't believe she thought I was jealous of her. I realized now that everyone changes. I just hope I didn't, but then again, maybe it was time for me to make a change.

Dealing with Nicole and her attitude, I didn't take time out to enjoy the moment. I was on an airplane everyday doing shows in a different city every night. I felt great about the tour and was very excited to be a part of it. I was also still a little star-struck by Slyy and Janice, but I knew it would wear off soon.

"How are the rehearsals going with Nicole?" Garrett asked.

"What rehearsals?" I responded with an attitude.

"What do you mean by that?" He asked.

"I'm no longer working with Nicole because she's tired of rehearsing," I replied, then went on to tell him about the conversation I had with her.

Garrett was shocked. "Nicole has gotten a touch of the limelight. It happens to people, and she will regret it."

The next day, Slyy's manager called to inform me of a pay rate change. When I heard this, I got upset, thinking they were going to lower our pay. Instead, he stated our pay rate would increase. Once the tour started, we would get paid $2000 a week and $300 Per Diem.

We would get paid $1200 per week for rehearsal and $150 Per Diem. The per diem was less when we were rehearsing because we could go to a grocery store and purchase food to cook, which was something you couldn't do on the road.

"Are you serious?" I yelled into the telephone, feeling like I had hit the lottery.

"Yes. Is there a problem?" The manager asked, thinking I wasn't happy with the pay change.

"No, I'm excited we're getting paid such a high rate."

This would be the most money I had ever gotten for dancing. Now I knew why people were addicted to the business. It was because of the money, and this was only the beginning.

I finally decided to quit my job and take a chance. It was very hard for me to leave after working there for over three years. However, I wouldn't be able to go home because we were going to start rehearsal soon.

After calling my boss to resign, I was no longer employed by PPC Marketing. It was terrifying yet thrilling, and it made me realize I had to make my dancing career work.

Although Nicole had already quit her job, I didn't want to make a decision so quickly. Since everything seemed to be working out, I became more comfortable with my decision. With the money I would be making from the tour, I would have a nice savings account and be financially stable once the tour was over.

Slyy rented me and Nicole one-bedroom apartments in Los Angeles to live while we rehearsed. The apartments were fully furnished and set up for people staying a short time. It was like being in a hotel with room and maid service and all the amenities.

I felt like I had died and gone to heaven with all the first-class treatment. I never would have thought this was how dancers lived. I also understood that Slyy treated his dancer very differently from other artist and that this wasn't the normal perks for dancers. Needless to say, I didn't ever want it to end.

Slyy also arranged for a car service to drive us to and from rehearsals. We would be rehearsing for the tour Monday through Friday, and were off on the weekends.

Rehearsing for eight hours a day, five days a week was like working a nine-to-five job. The only difference is this was something I loved to do. I couldn't wait for rehearsals to start. I was ready.

CHAPTER 12

The car service was at our apartment early and ready to take Nicole and I to rehearsal. We were eager to get started but didn't say much to each other. Blanca was already in the dance studio with another dancer when we arrived.

"Hey, Blanca," Nicole and I said.

She gave us a slight smile. This was her way of saying hello. Blanca and the other girl were acting very snooty towards us.

"Why is she staring at me?" Nicole asked.

The other dancer had a smirk on her face, and you could tell she didn't approve of us being there. Although I brushed her attitude off and tried to focus on why I was there, she was bothering Nicole.

"What are you looking at?" Nicole said to the dancer.

"Are you talking to me?" The dancer asked.

"Yes, I'm talking to you. Do you have a problem?" Nicole responded.

The dancer walked over to Nicole and got right up in her face. "I have a problem with you because you don't belong here. You're a ghetto, wanna-be dancer."

When Nicole pushed her out of her face, the dancer swung and hit Nicole so hard on the side of her head, it made her stumble. Blanca and I tried to stop them before things really got out of hand.

"Calm down!" Blanca yelled.

"I will knock your ass out!" The dancer yelled.

"Do it!" Nicole yelled back.

It took us a minute to try and get them to settle down. I took Nicole out of the room and talked to her so she could relax. After ten minutes, she was finally calm and ready to work without wanting to fight.

By the time we walked back into the studio, the other dancer seemed to have calmed down, also. They stayed on one side of the room and we stayed on the other. As we waited for rehearsal to start, we sat in complete silence, as Blanca and her friend laughed and talked.

Blanca took more time trying to be seen by Slyy and remain in the spotlight that she forgot about the true feeling of dancing. It wasn't about dancing to her. It was about how many jobs she could get, how much money she could make, and how popular she could become.

For me, it was an opportunity of a lifetime to be paid to do something I loved. Nothing else mattered to me; I just wanted to dance. Once I left the stage, I returned to my normal life.

The thrill of dancing was becoming someone else on stage. I was back to normal myself after removing the makeup and costumes, but most dancers lived their life stage-ready every day.

Almost every performer has an alter ego. This gave you the courage to become someone else and entertain people. My alter ego name was Carmella, and when I became her on stage, I was a totally different person and embraced whatever costume I was wearing and dance moves I was doing.

The door opened to the dance studio and Queen, the choreographer walked in. Nicole and I looked at each other and laughed to ourselves.

He had on fitted jeans, an Ed Hardy t-shirt with a matching hat, Ugg boots, some large Gucci sunglasses and purse, a scarf around his neck that was so long that it touched his knees and his face was completely covered in makeup. He finished his look off with fake eyelashes and entirely too much lip gloss.

Queen walked straight over to us, looked me up and down, smacked his lips, and said, “What’s your name?”

“Music.”

“My name is Queen,” he responded very nastily, “I’m the choreographer for Slyy’s tour. Do you have a problem with that?”

He stood in my face with his lips twisted up. He was so close that I could smell the strawberry gum he was chewing. I was confused by his question and tone. He heard that I had choreographed a routine for Slyy and wanted me to know that the gig was up.

“I didn’t expect to choreograph the show, but you really need to get out of my face,” I demanded.

Blanca and the other girl looked at me quite surprised. Most dancers would never say anything back to the choreographer because they thought talking back was disrespectful. I didn’t let people talk to me that way and I wasn’t going to allow it now.

I looked at Blanca and the other dancer and gave them a look that made them turn around. They already thought we were rough around the edges and now it was showing, but I didn’t care.

As Queen stared at me, I stared right back at him. I was not going to be intimidated and I wanted him to know he had met his match. After a few seconds of the stare down, he walked away and started rehearsal.

This was not how our first day of rehearsal was supposed to go. At first, I was so excited to get started, but now I was so ready to go home. He definitely made it a point to let me know he didn’t want me there, and I knew it would be a very long day.

Queen was a popular choreographer from New York who had worked with many music icons and was starting to work on Broadway musicals. He hired his friend Ashley, who was the person with Blanca when we arrived, to dance with us on Slyy’s tour.

Ashley was light-skinned, heavyset, and short with green eyes. Her long jet-black hair was straight with bangs. The first thing you noticed about her was her big, beautiful eyes.

Nicole and I were surprised they would hire someone overweight because most dancers were thin and in good shape. I liked her already because of her look, and loved that Slyy was hiring outside of the box and not just the typical dancer. I just wasn't feeling her personality.

Her long resume proved she could hang with the best. Once we saw her dance, we realized just how amazing she was. Ashley was feisty, and because she was friends with Queen, she spoke to him anyway she wanted to.

Ashley definitely knew who Nicole and I were, and she had the same disrespectful attitude that Blanca and Queen had towards us. The only reason they didn't respect us was because we were not trained dancers.

Blanca and Ashley had danced on tours and in music videos with almost every entertainer in the business, and they didn't respect anyone who hadn't done the same.

They had on heels, a face full of makeup, and tightly-fitted clothing. They looked like they were about to go out to a club instead of rehearsing.

Nicole and I came to rehearsal with baggy jogging pants, t-shirts, and gym shoes. Nicole had a bandana on her head and I wore a baseball hat. We definitely didn't fit in with their look.

Rehearsal started and Queen taught us several routines fast. He never stopped to see if Nicole and I were catching on. Queen's choreography was very technical and challenging. So, I had to focus to make sure I got it.

He had a totally different style of dancing than what we were used to. It helped that I was such a quick learner. Queen made sure he was rude to us the entire rehearsal and continued to rush through the routines.

"Can you show me that eight count again?" Nicole asked him.

"No!" Queen snapped and kept teaching.

It was obvious Blanca and Ashley already knew the routines because they did them effortlessly. Queen had a mean look on his face when we couldn't catch up with the choreography.

"If you don't like how I'm teaching, than leave," he kept telling us.

"What?" Nicole asked, annoyed.

"You guys are not ready. If you were trained dancers, you could catch on to the routines," Queen said with a smirk on his face.

I was frustrated because he was right. It was hard to keep up with his choreography. He used dancer terminology because he knew we didn't understand. He spoke in this foreign language the whole day, and I knew he would keep using it at every rehearsal just to make his point. I might not have known the terminology, but I could see him do the move, which was all I needed.

"Can you slow down so I can catch on to the moves?" I asked.

"No!" He said again.

"Why won't you show us the routines?" Nicole asked.

"I am showing you. You just can't catch on," he replied, while snickering.

It took everything inside of me to control my anger. I refused to let Queen make me feel uncomfortable. I knew I had skills and that should be all that mattered.

I wanted to call Garrett to let him know about the torture we were receiving from Queen, but decided to wait a couple of days to see if things would change. Maybe he would eventually warm up to us.

However, a few days passed and nothing changed. So, it was time to make that call. I felt like a kid telling on Queen, but I needed to do something about situation. This was supposed to be fun, and because of him it wasn't. He was ruining my dreams.

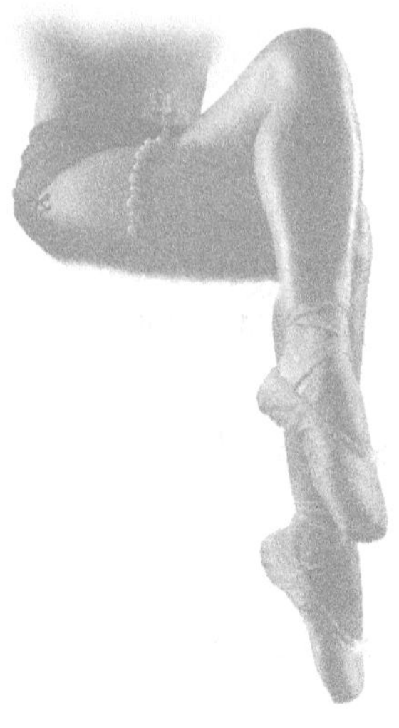

CHAPTER 13

“I need to speak with Slyy,” I told Garrett.

“What do you need, Music?”

“I really would like to talk directly to Slyy. Please. It’s important.”

Garrett could tell in my voice that I was very upset and something was wrong, so he didn’t question me any longer.

“I will see if Slyy is available to talk to you.”

“Thanks, Garrett.”

He never responded and abruptly hung up. An hour later, Slyy called me.

“Queen is treating us horribly at rehearsals. He doesn’t want us here, and he won’t teach us the routines. He only teaches the other dancers,” I blurted out as soon as I heard Slyy’s voice. I was so disappointed and stressed that he could hear it in my voice.

“Calm down, Music,” Slyy said in a relaxed tone.

“Okay, I’m calm.”

“I hired you and Nicole, and I’m the only one who can fire you. Queen doesn’t have any authority on this tour.”

“But we can’t learn the routines because he won’t teach us.”

“Try to deal with Queen. I know he can be a lot to handle, but he’s the best. Don't let him stop you from learning. He's just giving you a hard time," Slyy replied very casually.

He was used to dealing with people like Queen. It was common for him in this business, but it wasn't for me.

"Can you handle Queen?" Slyy asked.

"I guess," I responded.

"You're stronger than that. If you can't handle him, you can't handle this business," Slyy said.

"I can handle him," I replied with confidence.

"Good. That's what I wanted to hear. Now go to rehearsal and learn those routines, because you're too sexy to be stressing out."

"Okay," I said softly.

I felt good after I finished talking with Slyy. Our conversation was short but very effective, and I knew my job was secure. Now that I knew Queen couldn't fire me, I was going to have a different attitude and not let him annoy me.

~~~~~~~

Four days of rehearsing and we had already learned four routines. Queen was moving fast and constantly making me angry.

"We're going to learn a new routine today. Can you girls handle that?" Queen asked me and Nicole.

We didn't say a word.

"If I was able to hire the dancers, we would be done by now. You guys are slowing me down," Queen said, displeased.

He knew Slyy was very persistent about Nicole and I being a part of his tour, and he hated it. He wanted to make sure we didn't catch on to his choreography so Slyy would fire us. He moved through routines fast, while continuing to be rude.

Slowly, I felt my confidence slipping away. I knew I needed to refocus and start fighting for my spot on this tour. I had worked too hard to let
~~~~~~~

Queen try to take the opportunity away from me. My anger was helping me learn the dance routines.

"This is my assistant, Lisa, and she will be teaching you some choreography today," Queen said, as he introduced her to us.

"Hey, girl," Blanca and Ashley said, while running to hug her.

"Hey, guys," Lisa said, greeting me and Nicole.

"Hey," we both said.

Queen was not a hip-hop dancer, and he definitely was not going to let me help him with the hip-hop routine. He never commented about the song I choreographed, but he stole my show concept and a few dance moves for the tour. Queen choreographed all the slow tempo songs, while Lisa choreographed the upbeat songs.

While rehearsing, Lisa started off being nice to us, and then she would have an attitude once in a while. By now, we were prepared and expected this from her.

Lisa was a hip-hop choreographer, but her method of teaching was very different from the typical way. I noticed that after Lisa finished teaching us the routines, she started doing them with us and made a spot for herself.

This was beyond teaching; she had become one of the dancers. It was obvious Queen brought Lisa in to replace me or Nicole.

Since he only brought one dancer, I knew he was trying to get rid of only one of us. Seeing that I had the routines down and Nicole didn't, I wasn't worried about being replaced. Nicole, on the other hand, was in a bad position. She couldn't do any routines without making tons of mistakes.

Queen always had Lisa dancing in the middle of us. Lisa and I were hitting every move, and we looked great together, which made Nicole stand out in the worse way. I'm not sure if Nicole knew she looked horrible or if she even cared.

We had three weeks of rehearsals left and all of the choreography was done. The only thing left to do was rehearse with the band, get fitted for our outfits, and rehearse on stage.

I was embarrassed for Nicole, but she was the least of my worries. I needed to make sure I was on point and could keep up with the other dancers. At rehearsals, I never did the choreography full out, just enough to let them know I had it.

I wanted Queen to think he was going to get me fired because of my dancing. So, I continued to hold back on my skills until the time was right.

~~~~~~~

Two weeks passed and we were still rehearsing. Lisa was very friendly with me and kept making small talk all morning.

"How do you like Los Angeles so far?" She asked me.

"It's okay. I haven't seen much," I responded.

"I will show you around town sometimes."

"Thanks. That would be cool," I said, wondering why she was being so nice.

She never had any conversations with me before. For some reason, Blanca and Ashley weren't being as rude to me either. It was a strange day, but nice to have a break from their constant impoliteness.

I noticed that Blanca, Lisa, and Ashley were dressed up with more makeup than usual and looked like they just came from the beauty shop. They looked like they were ready to go on stage to perform.

"Let's get started ladies," Queen quickly said, as he walked in the studio.

We went through all the routines several times. He was a little more strict than normal and was actually giving me directions. I kept looking at them like they were crazy. I didn't know if Nicole even picked up on how peculiar they were acting. She seemed not to be paying attention to anything lately.

Queen was also dressed up, not in his normal jeans, fitted t-shirt, and scarf. The way they were dressed made Nicole and I look like we had just gotten out of the bed and came straight to rehearsal without caring about
~~~~~~~

our appearance.

"Music, move over a little to the center. Blanca, your turns are off," Queen said very seriously. "Let's do it again."

In the middle of our routine, Slyy, Janice, Garrett, and his security guards walked in. It was now obvious what was going on. When I saw Slyy and his entourage, I immediately became furious, because if I knew they were coming, I would have dressed a little better.

Once again, Queen was still trying to make us look terrible, and he succeeded this time. I was so upset that I had to compose myself. I felt embarrassed, especially since they looked stage-ready and I was looking like a homeless person.

With all this going on, I still don't think Nicole even cared how she looked. She was so wrapped up in the limelight that she couldn't see what was happening.

"Stop the music and start from the beginning," Garrett instructed.

Queen turned the music off, walked over to Slyy and started talking to him. Then he called Lisa over and introduced her to Slyy and Janice.

"Come and say hello," Slyy said, signaling for us.

"I'm sorry I'm not dressed up. I wasn't informed you were coming today," I said with an attitude.

Slyy frowned. "I told Queen I was coming today and to tell you guys."

"Well, I guess he forgot to tell us, but he did tell the dancers he wanted to know," I replied, looking at Blanca, Ashley, and Lisa.

Slyy looked at Queen and raised his eyebrow because now he knew what I told him was true. He seemed bothered that Queen didn't relay his message.

In a frustrated voice, Slyy told Queen, "Let me see the routines."

Queen jumped up and said, "Get in position."

I knew it was show time. We went to our positions and waited for the music to start. My heart was pounding and I started breathing fast. I was getting nervous and my adrenaline was pumping, but I wasn't going to let my nerves get the best of me.

With their eyes locked on us, Slyy and his crew were ready to see what we had been working on. When the music started, I closed my eyes, took a deep breath, and pretended I was on stage in front of millions of people. It was time for me to show Queen what I'd been holding back.

We were in the middle of the routine, and by the look on Queen's face, he was stunned by my performance. He never saw me dance like that before and was surprised to see I could hang with the other dancers. I enjoyed looking at the expression on his face. He couldn't deny that I was dancing my butt off.

Nicole started making so many mistakes that she couldn't catch back on to the routine. She stuck out like a sore thumb, while Lisa and I had a great connection and moved in unison.

You could see the look on Slyy and his entourage's faces as they watched Nicole look like a fool. We had been rehearsing for months, so there was no reason she should not have had the routines by now. Slyy looked completely disappointed.

In the middle of the last routine, Slyy and his crew left without saying a word. A short while later, Garrett came back in the room and announced that rehearsal was over.

"Garrett, what just happened?" Queen asked nervously.

Garrett looked at us and walked out the dance studio without giving him an explanation.

"Okay, I guess rehearsal is over." Queen said.

"What do you think is going on?" Lisa asked.

"Honey, I don't know. Just get your shit and go," Queen said.

Before Queen walked out of the room, he walked over to me and whispered in my ear, "Music, I knew you were a fabulous dancer."

"I guess you don't have to be a trained dancer to be amazing," I said.

"Bitch, you were holding out on me," Queen smiled and winked at me, as he walked out of the room.

I finally gained his respect, but was left wondering if I still had a job.

~~~~~~~

After the short two hours of rehearsal, I returned to my apartment confused. I put on some pajamas, turned the television on, sat on the bed, and started thinking of reasons why Slyy would walk out of our rehearsal.

I didn't know the answer, but knew. He wasn't happy, and that was something for me to be worried about. Ten minutes later, Nicole was knocking on my door.

"The way Slyy left rehearsal today has me scared. Can you please help me with the choreography?" Nicole asked as soon as I opened the door.

"Why did you wait so long to ask me for help?" I asked.

"I got caught up."

I started not to help her, but she looked so pitiful that I couldn't leave her hanging.

"I'll help you, but you need a lot of work."

I knew that if she hadn't gotten the routines in months, I couldn't teach her in one night.

"Thanks, Music."

"No problem. Now let's get started."

I thought to myself that I really needed to learn how to stand firm on my word. I said I wasn't going to help her, but there I was helping her again.

Before we started rehearsing, Nicole asked to use my bathroom. After five minutes, I knocked on the bathroom door to see if she was okay. She came out the bathroom quickly and was now ready to dance.

"What is that on your nose?" I asked.

"It's nothing," Nicole replied, wiping the white residue off.
~~~~~~~

"What were you doing in the bathroom?" I inquired.

"Nothing! Now let's dance," Nicole said, appearing energized.

"Were you doing drugs?"

"Don't be silly, Music. Let's dance," Nicole replied, while acting hyped up like she just finished drinking a cup of coffee.

I looked at Nicole and knew she had just snorted cocaine in my bathroom. I couldn't believe I didn't notice this before, but it would explain a lot of things.

"Nicole, do you do drugs?"

She never responded and acted like she was doing the routine without music playing.

"Nicole!" I shouted.

"What!"

"Did you just do drugs in my bathroom?" I yelled.

"Yes! What's the big deal?"

"I didn't know you did drugs."

"Music, I need it from time to time. It's the only way I can deal with my busy schedule. I need the energy to keep going."

"That's probably why you can't stay focused and learn these routines."

"Mind your business. Now are you going to show me the routines or not?"

I started showing her, but my mind was still focused on her doing drugs. We had only been rehearsing for a couple of hours before Nicole started complaining.

"I'm tired. I'm going back to my room."

"You're probably tired because your high is coming down."

"You're the one fucking up my high."

"You really should keep rehearsing if you want to get these moves."

"I'm done and going back to my room."

"Okay," I said nonchalantly.

I wasn't going to argue with her. I didn't know what she was thinking. Maybe she knew it was a lost cause. Nicole left and I shook my head in disbelief.

A few hours later, there was a knock on my door. I thought it was Nicole wanting to rehearse some more. Prepared to tell her to go to hell, I snatched the door open, but to my surprise, it was Slyy and Garrett.

"Hi," I said stunned.

"Can I talk to you?" Slyy asked with an irritated look on his face.

"Sure. Come in."

"I know I hired you and Nicole together, but I'm not happy with her performance. I've wasted time and money on her," Slyy stated.

I interrupted him. "I was working with her today."

"It doesn't matter. I've wasted enough time and need to move on with my tour."

"She looked dreadful today," Garrett added.

"Why hasn't she picked up the routines?" Slyy asked.

"She did a good job at the showcase. What happened?" Garrett inquired.

They were asking me so many questions I couldn't answer them quick enough. I told him that I had rehearsed with her for a month before the seminar and worked with her one-on-one.

"I have no choice but to fire Nicole," Slyy said, as I opened my eyes wide. "I hope you don't leave because of this."

"Of course not. We're not a package deal," I quickly replied, trying to save my job.

"I'm happy to hear that, because you did an awesome job today and I want you to be a part of my tour," Slyy said sincerely.

"Thank you for allowing me to work for you. I'm so happy to be here,"

I responded, as Slyy smiled.

"Transportation will continue to pick you up for rehearsals, but we will be rehearsing at a different location with the band," Garrett informed me.

Suddenly, sadness stole my joy for a moment. Although Nicole had gotten on my last nerve, I didn't want her to get fired.

"I'm sorry it had to happen this way. She has to be accountable for her actions. You couldn't help her," Slyy said, then walked out of my room.

"It's sad that she came this far and not work hard to stay here," Garrett added before closing the door behind him.

I will never know what got into Nicole. I did nothing but help her, but she didn't want it. She did it to herself. I tried to fight in the beginning to keep her on the tour, but her lack of dancing experience is what got her fired.

Nicole taught me a lesson. I vowed to always do my best and never let the fame go to my head. In this business, you can always be replaced.

The next day, the car was on time to pick me up and take me to rehearsal without Nicole. I arrived at the new location, where a mock stage was set up to look exactly like our real stage for the tour.

We were fitted for our show costumes and had a dress rehearsal with the band. Each song required a wardrobe change. Our outfits ranged from long flowing gowns with beautiful costume jewelry, to fitted body suits, and crop tops and hip-hugger pants.

We had very quick wardrobe changes during the show, so we definitely needed to rehearse. Slyy hired two assistants to help us with our clothing. We were also scheduled for a photo shoot the next day for the tour book.

I didn't realize how much work it took to organize a tour. The crew was building the set and the lighting staff was figuring out which lights to use. Our assistants were shopping for accessories, and Slyy's personal assistant was getting his clothes designed.

The managers were working directly with the promoters to book shows in different cities, and Slyy was doing promotional radio spots to advertise his upcoming tour.

Garrett was working closely with the promoter's staff to make sure the dressing rooms in every city had everything we requested. In each dressing room there had to be fruit, bottled water, crackers, cheese, and hot food.

There would be thirty-two people traveling on tour with us, four tour buses, and two large eighteen-wheeler trucks to carry the band equipment, lights, and stage props. This was a big production and a very expensive tour.

We only had minor problems to fix with our wardrobe changes. We had eight costume changes and had to change our entire outfit, including shoes and sometimes jewelry.

One of the wardrobe changes had to be done in thirty seconds. There was a method to everything. Our assistants played a major part in making sure we had on the correct costumes for the songs. They had our clothes laid out and ready for us each time we entered the dressing room.

We had a crew of five just to set up the band equipment, a light crew of three, a wardrobe crew, two assistants, hair stylists, make-up artists, and personal assistants.

After the dress rehearsal, Slyy had a meeting with everyone.

"I'm happy with the way the show is looking so far. I've added more shows and the tour will be extended to one year," Slyy announced.

We started jumping up and down and screaming. That meant we were going to be making money for a whole year straight.

Slyy added, "After we finish this one-year tour, we're going overseas for six months. We will be visiting places like Europe, Japan, and Germany. So, get your passports ready."

Slyy treated everyone with respect and valued our opinions. Everyone would travel the same way he does and stayed at five-star hotels.

He paid us triple the amount you would make with any other entertainers. People were dying to work with him, and we truly felt privileged to be chosen.

CHAPTER 14

After Slyy's new CD went double platinum, all the shows for the tour were quickly sold out. He worked with new producers on his album and credited his success to them. They created a new sound and recreated him.

Roger Rort was his birth name, but once he started working with the new producers, he started going by Slyy. He would always wear dark sunglasses, or if a woman was in his presence.

Everyone thought it was strange for him to be wearing dark sunglasses while indoors, but the producers knew he wore them so no one could see his eyes wandering.

The producers said he was always doing something devious, so they decided to call him Slyy. They called him this while he recorded his new CD, and by the time it was completed, everyone caught on to his new name.

His record company loved his new name and wanted to use it. Slyy changed the spelling to make it more unique, and from that point on, Roger Rort officially became "Slyy."

Along with the new album and name came a cool new style. Slyy was very versatile with his wardrobe, and his new look always kept his fans in suspense. He didn't want to be limited to one style, so he constantly switched his looks.

You never knew what he would be wearing next. He would wear a jogging suit with matching gym shoes and a baseball hat one day, and the next day, he would sport a tailor suit with the matching shoes and hat.

His fans loved his versatile look and always wanted to get a glimpse of what he was wearing. Slyy was re-created, restyled, and more famous than he had ever been.

He was in his late thirties, 6'1", light-skinned, short brown dreadlocks, grey eyes, a muscular body, and juicy lips. He was definitely eye candy. The women loved him and men felt intimidated by his looks. He looked like LL Cool J, Allen Payne, and Rick Fox all mixed up into one package.

A recovering alcoholic, Slyy had been sober for five years. He hit rock bottom while filming his last movie. One day he arrived on the set so drunk that he was talking loudly and yelling at everyone. The director tried to tell him to go and sleep it off, but Slyy refused.

Growing out of control, he started cursing the director out and tried to fight the crew. The director fired him on the spot and it was all over the news.

The next day after Slyy sobered up, he was so embarrassed that he tried to contact the director to apologize and get his job back. The director accepted his apology, but did not rehire him.

Instead, Slyy was replaced with a new younger actor. The movie went number one at the box office and made millions of dollars.

Although he didn't drink every day, whenever he got drunk he was loud, violent, and very demanding. His drunkenness was destroying his career until Janice helped him check into a rehabilitation center. Six months later, he was clean.

That's what made him take a break from acting and focus on his singing. Bad press will make you switch gears quickly.

CHAPTER 15

While taking a short break from sound check, I got a chance to talk to Slyy one on one. He sat down next to me to relax. This was something he did with all his employees. He didn't act like a celebrity around us. To him we were his family and he was just a normal person.

"I don't feel like you want my money or anything else from me. It's nice to talk to someone that speaks the truth all the time," Slyy said.

"I'm just being me," I responded.

"I hired you because you are a great dancer, new to the business and a breath of fresh air."

"I'm just happy to be dancing."

"I'll teach you how to succeed in this business," Slyy said.

"That would be great learning from someone like you."

"You haven't been burned by the business. It's ruthless, and if you're not careful, you will get caught up in it. The other dancers just want my money or a solo dance, but you really seem like you just want to dance."

"I do! I love dancing, and I want to experience life on the road," I eagerly replied.

"I will make sure you experience everything the road has to offer."

"My dad would be proud of me if he was alive. He really wanted me to accomplish my dreams."

"I'm sorry to hear about your father. Is your mother alive?" Slyy asked.

"Yes, she's alive, but she doesn't want me in the music industry. She wasn't happy when I told her that I was working with you. She wants me to be a lawyer. I'm the only child, so it's just me and my mom."

"Parents have their own dreams for their kids. She will come around one day."

"Do you have any kids?" I asked.

"I…I…I…"

"What's wrong, Slyy? You don't know if you have kids?" I asked, laughing.

"You know how that story goes. Don't ask, don't tell," Slyy said laughing.

"Okay, I won't ask."

"I've heard you singing at sound check. You have a great voice. Did your parents sing?"

"No, neither one of them can sing. I don't know where I got my voice from. I guess the same place my dancing skills came from. For some reason, it's all natural to me."

"Maybe I can help you with your singing career."

"Thanks, but I'm not interested in singing."

"With a voice like that, you need to be interested. A dancer that can sing can make a lot of money."

"I should start thinking about it since everyone keeps telling me to do something with my voice."

"Well, when you're ready, I would love to help you."

"Thanks. I will keep that in mind."

"Are you ready?" Garrett asked, interrupting our conversation.

"Yes, I'm ready. I'll talk to you later, Music."

Slyy was a very down-to-earth man and wanted everyone to succeed. People always wanted something from him and hung around him in hopes of becoming the next star.

The women around him were beautiful and spent all their time and money trying to look perfect, while the men spent their time and money trying to impress the women. This was getting old to Slyy.

"Everyone that's flying out tomorrow please be in the lobby on time. You have very early flights home," Garrett announced.

"While you're visiting your family and friends, make sure you recharge yourself. I want you ready for this tour when you return," Slyy said to everyone.

~~~~~~~

With only a few days off before the tour started, I went home to pack and get my personal business in order since I would be gone for a year. I missed my apartment and was happy to be home. Before I could get my luggage through the door, my telephone was ringing.

"I was checking to see if you made it home yet," my cousin Sydney said.

"I just walked through the door."

"I'm on my way over."

"See you soon."

I was excited to see Sydney, who was like the sister I never had. Since I was the only child, we hung out all the time. I often wished she was a dancer so we could work and travel together, but dancing was something she was not interested in doing.

Since my time at home was limited, I immediately started taking care of business so I would have time to spend with my friends and family. Since the last guy I was dating couldn't handle a long distant relationship I no longer had a boyfriend and was free and single.

I had already arranged for my friend to sublet my apartment while I was gone, and my car would stay parked in my garage until I returned.
~~~~~~~

Thirty minutes later, my cousin was at my house.

"How are you?" Sydney asked, giving me a big hug as soon as I opened the door.

"I'm good, just tired," I replied.

"I'm happy you're home," she said.

"Now let's go get something to eat," I told her.

"I'm sorry you've been having a hard time on the road, but it will get better."

Sydney knew about the things I was going through because I called her almost every night.

"I'm just glad you were available to talk. You have to come to one of our shows."

"I would love to attend one of your shows. I can't wait to get my hands on Slyy. He's so fine," she said.

"He's cool, but he's too old for you."

"He's not that old. He's only in his late thirties," she stated.

"We're both in our early twenties, so he's too old for you and me."

"Come on so we can go shopping and get you some hot clothes. You can't let those dancers out dress you," Sydney said, changing the subject.

"It's a good thing you know about fashion, because I wouldn't know what to buy," I said.

"That's why I'm here. So let's go, and make sure to bring your credit cards," Sydney said, as she smiled.

After grabbing my purse, we were out the door.

Hours later, I finally made it home. My apartment looked like I had purchased everything from every store we visited. It felt good to have Sydney do all the work and pick out designer clothes for me.

I looked like a different person in every outfit, and I would definitely fit in now. I purchased designer shoes, clothes, sunglasses, purses, makeup, perfume, lingerie, jewelry and some huge pieces of luggage.

Even though I was against wearing fake hair because my hair was already long, Sydney insisted I needed to look like a star, and since a majority of the stars wore wigs or hair weaves, she forced me to purchase a few wigs.

I don't know what I would have done without Sydney. She was a lifesaver, and I was now prepared to return to the tour with a new look. We had done so much in one day, yet I still had things to do.

I took the time to check my voicemail and had several messages from dancers wanting me to hook them up with a job with Slyy.

"They will never stop," I said out loud to myself.

Almost seven months had past and I hadn't spoken to Raven, who was still busy modeling. I didn't want to call her after her bizarre attitude at our last job together.

She seemed to be feeling herself and didn't need me anymore. The break from Raven actually made me feel stress free. Maybe we needed the time apart from each other.

It was Saturday morning and time for me to fly to Miami for the first show of the tour. I was over packed with five large pieces of luggage, but Sydney insisted I take those "*just in case*" items.

It was hard saying goodbye to my family. I wanted to stay longer, but I was also ready to dance, travel, and see the world. My family and friends were happy for me, but at the same time, they were sad because they wouldn't see me for a while.

The time had finally come for me to experience everything I ever dreamed of. My mom was still not supporting me. So, of course, she didn't want me to go back on tour with Slyy.

I didn't understand why she just couldn't be happy for me. Needless to say, I didn't talk to her much during my visit home because I knew she would only try to convince me to stay.

For the first part of the tour, we would be visiting many places including Miami, New Orleans, Atlanta, Detroit, St. Louis, Boston, Washington, Dallas, Minneapolis, California, Las Vegas, Chicago, Indiana, and Phoenix. We would go to many more cities before the tour ended, and then we would head overseas.

"Take care," Sydney sadly said.

"I will," I responded with the same sadness.

"I'm always here if you need to talk."

"I will call you all the time with updates on the tour," I assured her.

"You look great. Now go and show them the new and improved you," Sydney said proudly.

"I feel like a new person. Thanks for hooking me up."

Sydney made me look like a million bucks, and when I stepped out of the car at the airport, everyone was looking and trying to figure out who I was.

"Have a safe flight," Sydney said, as she waved goodbye.

"Thanks. I'll call you when I get to Miami."

Ready to start the tour, I checked my luggage in at baggage claim and headed for the gate. I didn't know what to expect, but I knew I was going to have the time of my life.

CHAPTER 16

After arriving safely, I met up with the dancers, band members, and crew at baggage claim. The few days off was much needed for everyone. We seemed happy to see each other, or at least pretended to be. Miami was sunny, hot, and absolutely beautiful.

This was my first time in Miami, so I was ready to put my bikini on and hit the beach. The band members were ready to meet women, and the dancers wanted to go to the bar to have a drink.

Vans were waiting outside the airport's exit to transport us to our hotel, and once we arrived in South Beach, I noticed a lot of green things on the outside wall of the hotel.

"What are those?" I asked the driver.

He replied, "Those are just lizards."

"Lizards!" I screamed.

"After it rains, the lizards come out. Don't worry, they'll leave when it rains again," the driver explained, but it didn't make me feel better.

"Where do they go?" I asked, concerned.

"I'm not sure. It usually rains for ten minutes, and when the sun comes back out, so does the lizards," the driver said.

I finally found the courage to leave the van and enter the hotel. I was so afraid a lizard was going to jump on me, so I rushed into the hotel. Inside, the hotel staff was extremely nice and gave us the royal treatment, which took my mind off the lizards for the moment.

One of the biggest benefits of traveling with Slyy was you were guaranteed to be treated like a star. Each of us had our own hotel room because he didn't believe in adults sharing rooms.

I walked into my stylish room, and it was beautiful. I had a king-size bed with an amazing white duvet, four large down-feathered pillows, a faux brown blanket at the bottom of the bed, a large suede embroidered headboard, a brown suede couch and chair, and breathtaking art hanging on the wall.

The bathroom was wonderful, with a Jacuzzi tub with separate shower, granite countertops, and heated lamps. There were flat-screen televisions in the bedroom area, bathroom, and sitting area. The balcony wrapped around the room with a magnificent view of the ocean.

There was a huge welcome basket waiting for me that I couldn't wait to dive into. It contained expensive gourmet chocolates, champagne, wine, cheeses, crackers, a plush robe, matching slippers, and wonderful scented candles. I was impressed.

Two hours later after getting settled in my room, Garrett called. "Slyy is taking everyone to Walt Disney World since the show isn't until tomorrow. You have thirty minutes to get ready and meet us in the lobby."

After taking a quick shower and touching up my makeup and hair, I changed into a pair of white jean shorts, a white fitted diamond studded tank top, a Gucci purse, cute wedge sandals and large dark sunglasses.

When I got to the lobby, none of the other dancers or band members was there. I waited, thinking everyone was late, but then started getting worried that they had left me.

Five minutes later, Slyy, Garrett, Janice, and the security guards stepped off the elevator.

Garrett walked up to me and said, "Wow, you look great! Looks like you had a makeover. Are you ready to go?"

"Where is everyone?" I asked.

"You're the only one going. Slyy wants to welcome you to the tour and take you to have some fun," Garrett replied.

"Come on, Music, let's go enjoy ourselves," Janice said, as she grabbed my arm and headed for the door.

"Thanks for taking me with you, guys."

"No problem," Janice said, while we got into the limousine.

The limo took us to the airport, where we boarded a private jet to Orlando. Once we arrived, we were greeted and personally escorted around by the park's security.

When people started recognizing Slyy, they never stopped bugging him for pictures and autographs. Slyy's appearance was making people go crazy.

Security quickly put us in a room until everything calmed down. Mickey Mouse came in to entertain us, take pictures, and make us feel like kids again. At night, we watched the parade of lights, which was magical just like the commercials said it would be.

Janice and I were having a great time. As we talked, I realized she was really cool.

"I'm excited to be working with you guys, but sometimes I feel a little intimidated by everyone," I said.

I was the youngest and the least experienced on the tour. Janice was a little older than Slyy and in her early 40's, but could easily pass for being in her 20's. Slyy never told anyone his age, but everyone thought he was in his late 30's.

"Don't worry about it. You have skills, and no one can take that away from you. Stick with me and you'll be fine," Janice told me.

"I'm happy to have someone to talk to because I feel all alone."

"Music, you're family now. You're never alone," Janice replied, then gave me a big hug.

"Thanks, Janice."

Janice was my new friend on the road and I admired her. She was beautiful inside and out. She had keen features, with big brown eyes, long eyelashes, full lips, large cheeks, and a shape to die for. She stood 5'8" with major junk in her trunk and a waistline so small I didn't think she had one.

The movie industry loved her exotic look and this helped her get hired for movie roles. She was a fantastic actress, very stylish, and dressed very hip. I knew I could learn a lot from her.

After hanging out at Walt Disney World all day, Slyy took us to dinner before we boarded the private jet back to Miami. At the dinner table, Slyy and Janice announced that they were adopting me as their daughter.

"Okay, Mom and Dad," I said, as everyone laughed.

Since they didn't have any kids, they took me under their wing and treated me like a real family member, which made me more relaxed. They wanted to keep me close to them and show me the ropes. This made it much easier for me to deal with life on the road.

"I thank you guys," I told them.

"You're a great person, Music, and new to the business. We want to protect you from the crazy people in the industry. You don't have to worry about anything now. You're family," Slyy said, as he put a spoonful of chocolate soufflé in his mouth.

CHAPTER 17

We were just finishing sound check and had three hours before the first show of the tour.

"Everything sounds and looks good, so let's have a great show tonight. Now head back to the hotel to get ready," Slyy said into the microphone.

Since there were no problems at sound check, we were done within one hour. That was perfect because the longer the sound check, the more it cut into our time to rest and prepare before the show. Sometimes sound check could feel like a rehearsal, and by the time you made it back to your room, you were worn out.

On the ride back to the hotel, they announced on the radio that the tickets to Slyy's show were sold out within two hours. I started feeling the excitement in the pit of my stomach. Resting was now the last thing on my mind because I wanted to take my time getting dressed to make sure I looked perfect.

I took a hot bath to relax and unwind. I put my makeup on first, with fake lashes, foundation, eye shadow, and the works. I put a few curls in my hair, and with the help of the weave, my hair looked much longer and fuller.

After putting on four-inch, ankle-strap heels with a beautiful short dress, I took a quick look in the mirror and I looked like a star.

Not wanting to be late and have Garrett on my ass, I grabbed my bag and purse and headed to the lobby of the hotel. With the show scheduled to start at seven o'clock, everyone had to meet in the lobby at five o'clock. Everyone was on time and seemed just as excited as I was.

When we pulled up to the backstage door of the venue, it was crowded and congested. My heart started pounding from the thought of performing in front of all those people.

Once we finally entered the building, Garrett instructed us on where our dressing rooms were and what time we needed to be "stage ready". Garrett was very strict about being dressed on time.

He wanted us to be completely dressed in our first outfit with our makeup on and waiting for him to escort us to the stage.

There were so many people and celebrities backstage, I almost ran into a wall trying to look at everyone. I really wanted to fit in, so I tried to act like it didn't bother me. When we walked into the backstage area with Slyy, everyone stopped and moved to let us by.

The way everyone was dressed in our entourage made us look very important people. This was totally different from the shows I used to do. I was used to coming to the shows in jeans or jogging suits, but this felt very different and I liked it.

We entered our dressing room, which was set up exactly as we requested it to be. After putting down our bags, we started getting ready for the show.

"Did you guys see all the entertainers backstage?" Lisa asked.

"Girl, this place is filled with money!" Blanca said, excited.

I sat in silence as they made small talk with each other, not trying to include me.

"Let's rock this first show. You know how we do it," Ashley said.

"No, I don't know how you do it," I whispered to myself.

"You have thirty minutes to show time," Garrett announced as he knocked on our door. In his language that meant to start getting dressed.

The next time Garrett knocked, he said, "You have fifteen minutes to show time." That meant make sure you have your entire outfit on and finish your stretching.

All stretching had to be done in the dressing room because Slyy's rule was when we left the dressing room, we should be ready to hit the stage.

Garrett opened our dressing room door without knocking and said, "Five minutes to show time, ladies." This meant you should have your outfit and shoes on, makeup and hair done, and be ready to go.

Five minutes later, he yelled, "It's show time!" This meant you better be walking out of your dressing room or he would be furious.

Garrett and the security guards escorted us to the stage area, where we waited for Slyy. I had never been so nervous before in my life. You could hear the crowd clapping and screaming, and the lights were turned down to let the audience know the show was about to start.

I peeked at the audience; it was extremely packed. The other dancers and band members were laughing and talking with each other, while I stood there by myself waiting to go on stage.

With all the excitement, I also felt sadness. It was horrible to feel left out, but I had to get used to it because we had a long tour ahead of us. I didn't have anyone to enjoy this with.

After Slyy was escorted by security to the stage area, we held hands while Garrett said a prayer.

After the prayer, he said, "Burn up the stage and have a great show!"

Garrett gave the band the cue to go on stage and the crowd went crazy. The band started playing and the lights started flashing.

When Slyy walked onto the stage, we followed behind him. The crowd went wild when they saw Slyy in a red suit, while we had on silver long-flowing gowns. Once he started singing, we ripped our long gowns off to reveal the red, fitted short outfits we had on underneath.

When Slyy removed his jacket, he had on a more casual looking outfit with red accents. He didn't like wearing suits, but he wore one for the introduction of his show. Then he took it off to be more comfortable.

Even though the dancers didn't talk to me much, on stage, we performed like we were the best of friends. We smiled and laughed with each other the entire show.

The show ended with only minor problems from the sound, but the audience didn't even notice it and wanted an encore. Everyone felt good as we walked off the stage.

As much as I anxiously anticipated the first show, I was happy it was over. With non-stop dancing in heels for two hours, my feet were hurting and my body was aching.

We went back to the hotel and prepared to be in the lobby the next morning at five o'clock to catch a flight to the next city on the tour.

Everything was going good so far. I had the best time on stage and couldn't wait to do it again. I knew touring the world would be great.

~~~~~~~

Second shows were being added to the tour in almost every city. We completed the first half by flying to every city and now we were about to finish the remainder of the tour traveling on a tour bus.

This would be my first time riding on a tour bus, and I was so frantic I couldn't control myself. To talk about my dreams was one thing, but to actually live them was unbelievable and now becoming a reality.

When the tour bus picked us up in Texas, everyone wanted to be the first person to claim their bed on the bus. I grabbed my video camera to capture the moment.

The dancers were riding on the bus with Slyy, Janice, Garrett, and the security guards. The band and crew had their own tour buses. Our bus was black with white designs on the outside. It was top-of-the-line with all the amenities.

When you walked on the bus, there was a couch on each side, wall-to-wall carpet, a flat-screen television, and a kitchen area with a refrigerator, microwave, sink, and a table for four.
~~~~~~~

The bathroom was small with marble floors and granite countertops; it also had a shower. When parked, one whole side of the bus extended to make the living room area larger.

Once you passed the bathroom, there were twelve bunk beds, six on each side. The bunk beds were very comfortable with down comforters and pillows, a curtain to shield your bed for privacy, a flip-down television with a DVD player, and your own personal fan and heater.

When you passed the bunk beds, there was a door that opened up to a one-bedroom master suite. The bedroom had a king-size bed with designer comforters and pillows, a wet bar, vanity mirror, closet, and a bathroom. I felt like I was in five-star hotel on wheels.

Bubba, who would be our personal driver for the entire tour, showed us how to work everything on the bus and gave us all the bus rules.

I selected the middle bunk since it was easy for me to get in and out. Some of the dancers said the middle bunk was the best bunk. The top bunk made you feel like you were going to fall off and you felt all the bumps in the road on the bottom bunk.

We had been on the road for two months, and the dancers were starting to warm up to me by making small talk. I knew the only reason they were trying to be cool with me was because they knew I was close with Slyy and Janice.

By now, I was used to them and their bitchiness, and it didn't bother me anymore. I dealt with them just like they dealt with me, as purely a working relationship.

I hung out a lot with Janice while we were on the road. She was the only person I wanted to be around. Of course, the other dancers had a problem with our friendship. Janice didn't hang out with anyone else, and she stayed on the tour with Slyy until it was time to film her next movie. Touring with him gave her something to do.

Slyy and Janice were in love, and were always hugging and whispering in each other's ears. They seemed like such a happy couple. Slyy even proposed to Janice before the tour started by giving her a ten-carat platinum diamond ring.

Janice had been working on the wedding plans and trying to get Slyy to pick a day for the wedding. With Janice trying to plan a wedding with such a challenging career, made it difficult for her to organize her special day.

Hanging out with Janice while on tour gave me something to do and I didn't feel so lonely. It was fun talking to her about the wedding plans and helping her with ideas. It was going to be a star-studded event and very expensive.

They were inviting over three hundred people, and it was going to be held at the Four Seasons Hotel in Beverly Hills, California. Janice's wedding dress cost twenty-five thousand dollars and Slyy's tuxedo was being custom made by a well-known designer.

It felt good to be surrounded by people with money, but also depressing because it wasn't my money. Still, I was just happy to have someone to talk to on the tour.

CHAPTER 18

"Ladies, I have a job for you. I want you to dance for a new song I'm adding to the show. I want you to be eye candy for the men. So, dance sexy with little movement," Slyy said, instructing me and Lisa.

"It's about time," Lisa said.

"It will be like dancing inside an Oreo cookie," Slyy said, smiling.

Since Lisa and I were both dark-skinned we would make the cookies, while he was the filling because he was light-skinned.

Blanca and Ashley were already dancing together on a couple of songs, so it was our time to shine.

"Can you guys handle that?" Slyy asked.

"No problem," I said.

"Of course," Lisa arrogantly responded.

Our first time performing together was eventful, and Lisa thought we were competing against each other. She was kicking, splitting, and dancing all around Slyy on stage.

She desperately tried to be noticed. I didn't feel the need to compete with her because I knew Slyy didn't want us to do a lot on stage.

I continued dancing sexy and seductively, while Lisa jumped around like a funky chicken on crack. When we got off stage, Lisa was heavily panting and sweating.

"You need to calm down," Garrett told Lisa.

"Why? What was wrong with my performance?" Lisa asked snippily.

"You're not doing what Slyy asked you to do," he said, aggravated by Lisa's tone.

"I was amazing and working it stage," Lisa responded.

"Well, you just keep working it and see how far that gets you," Garrett replied, while looking at her with frustration written all over his face.

Every show, Lisa continued to dance wildly on stage, and Garrett had grown tired of warning her.

"You're not dancing with Music anymore," Garrett told Lisa one night after one of her crazy performances.

"Why not?" Lisa asked.

"I tried to tell you to calm down, but you wouldn't listen to me," Garrett said.

"Slyy didn't tell me to stop dancing," Lisa snapped back.

"Honey, you need to act like I'm Slyy. He tells me what he wants you to know, and I relay the message."

Lisa didn't respond. Instead, she took a deep breath and blew it out hard.

"He's upset that you wouldn't do what he asked you to do on stage, so he told me to take you off the song."

"This isn't fair. So Music is going to dance on the song by herself?" Lisa asked with an attitude.

"Yes. You gave Music her own solo," Garrett said with a smile on his face.

He knew how Lisa treated me. Therefore, it felt good for him to say this to her.

"I'm a much better dancer than she is. I should be the one doing the solo dance," Lisa said.

"You can dance solo, just not on the stage with Slyy," Garrett replied with a smirk.

"I'm going to talk to Slyy about this," she said, then walked away headed for his dressing room.

"You better not disturb him with this," Garrett told her while following her.

"Slyy, what's going on?" Lisa said after opening his dressing room door without knocking.

Before Slyy could say anything, Garrett was right behind her, while I peeked inside the door to listen to the conversation.

"I know you didn't just open his door without knocking," Garrett said, as Lisa realized that she was out of line.

"I'm so sorry, Slyy. I wasn't thinking," Lisa said.

"It's fine. Come in and sit down. It must be very important for you to come in my room uninvited," Slyy told her, while sitting on the couch and drinking Hennessey on the rocks.

Slyy had fallen off the wagon and started back to heavily drinking alcohol again. He was now drinking before and after every show.

Irritated, Garrett sat down beside Lisa.

"I don't like people walking into my room unannounced. Where are my security guards?" Slyy asked Garrett.

"They are escorting Janice around backstage. They should be done in about fifteen minutes," he told Slyy.

"We need to hire more security. Who's going to watch my back? I can't keep sharing them with Janice." Slyy said.

"I will get right on it," Garrett said.

"Now what's the problem that made you open my door without knocking?" Slyy asked Lisa in a relaxed voice.

"I wanted to know why I can't dance on the song with Music," she asked nervously.

“Because you didn’t give me what I asked for.”

“I was trying to add some flavor,” Lisa nervously said.

“But you didn’t give me what I wanted,” Slyy said.

”I tried to tell you that, Lisa,” Garrett interrupted.

“I like to get what I want,” Slyy said seriously, looking directly at Lisa.

“I’m a much better dancer than Music and I’ve been in this business longer than she has. She doesn’t deserve a solo dance,” Lisa voiced, rolling her eyes at Garrett.

“You were the one jumping around on stage like a fool. You could still be dancing if you had followed directions,” Garrett said emphatically.

“I’m a trained dancer and Music isn’t,” Lisa added, rather upset.

“This has nothing to do with Music. You did this to yourself,” Slyy replied, while still sipping on his drink.

Lisa never responded.

“I’m done with this conversation. Goodbye,” Slyy finally said, then gestured for her to leave his room.

Lisa left quickly, rushing past me without saying a word.

The next day after the show, Lisa caught Slyy while he was walking to his dressing room. “Can I talk to you?”

“Sure come into my room,” Slyy said, as he wiped the sweat from his forehead after finishing another successful show.

Once again, I followed behind them to peek in the room to listen to what Lisa was going to say.

“Have a seat,” he told her, then poured some Vodka into a glass. “What’s on your mind?” He asked, while taking a sip of his drink.

“Music doesn’t look good dancing on the song by herself. She’s not experienced enough to capture the audience’s attention like I can.”

“Oh really,” Slyy said, astounded.

“She can’t deliver,” Lisa added.

"She looks good on stage to me," he said as he started feeling the buzz from his drink.

"I can find you another dancer."

"Why do I need another dancer?"

"You need a new dancer to replace Music."

"Why?"

"You need to have more experienced dancers working for you."

"What's all of this about, Lisa? You're really fucking up my high."

"I don't like Music."

"Do you think I'm going to fire Music in the middle of my tour because you don't like her?"

"Umm," Lisa said, feeling uncomfortable.

"What did Music do to you to make you not like her?"

"She's not a trained dancer and doesn't have a lot of experience."

"You sound crazy," Slyy said. Then he opened his dressing room door and yelled, "Music, come to my room now!"

I jumped to the side of the door trying not to be seen. I walked into Slyy's dressing room as if I didn't know what was going on. When I saw Lisa sitting there with a weird look on her face, I asked, "What's up?"

Slyy looked at Lisa and said, "Lisa doesn't think you look good dancing on the song by yourself."

I didn't respond, but instead gawked at Lisa.

"Music is a part of my family, and she's not going anywhere. You've been trying to get her fired, and it doesn't make sense," Slyy said, as Lisa put her head down.

"You can stop wasting your time. If you come back into my dressing room with any more bullshit, I will fire you on the spot. Do you understand?" Slyy asked her, while still drinking his Vodka.

"I understand," Lisa said.

I looked at her, shook my head, and simply said, "You are a piece of work," before walking out of the room livid.

When I returned to our dressing room, Lisa followed me and tried to explain her side of the story. I knew she needed her job, so she was trying to fix the situation. I felt good that Slyy had my back. Now I knew the dancers wouldn't bother me anymore.

I wasn't feeling Lisa, but I knew how to have a working relationship. I would be friends with her on the road to keep the peace, but that's where our friendship would end.

"Music, please believe that I wasn't trying to get you fired."

"Whatever Lisa."

"Music, I'm serious. Slyy took it the wrong way."

"No problem. Let's leave it alone. I'm cool," I told her so she could stop lying.

"You sure you cool?"

"Yes, I'm fine."

"Good, because I don't want you to think I was trying to get you fired," Lisa said, as she let out a breath of air.

I knew the truth and didn't care what she said. I just wanted her to shut up.

CHAPTER 19

We were six months into the tour and things were moving along smoothly. We had been riding on the bus for hours, and I was ready to relax in a hotel room. In the beginning, I couldn't wait to ride on the tour bus, but now the thrill was gone and I was ready to get off.

Sometimes we didn't even have hotel rooms. We would have to go straight to the venue and shower there before the show. Then we left immediately after the show to travel to the next city. After a week of this, I was ready to take a break from the tour bus.

We arrived in Detroit and checked into a unique and beautiful hotel. All of the hotel rooms were suites, so you were guaranteed it would be extraordinary. The room had a sunken living room, flat-screen televisions, and a huge king-size bed.

After walking into my suite, I ran and jumped on the bed, happy to be in a hotel. Next, I took a bath, ordered room service, and planned to relax on our night off. I lay down to get some much-needed rest and was asleep for two hours, when there was a knock on my door. When I opened it, Garrett walked in.

"Are you alone?" Garrett asked.

"Yes. Why?" I asked, while yawning.

"Slyy wants to talk to you."

"About what?"

"I don't know. Stop asking so many damn questions," he replied, annoyed.

His comment fully woke me up, and before I could respond, Slyy walked into my room.

"I'll be back shortly," Garrett said and then left quickly.

Thinking something was wrong, I started panicking.

Seeing the worried look on my face, Slyy said, "Come sit down next to me on the bed. Relax; nothing's wrong."

That was a relief to hear. Although he was family, a part of me still felt excited to be around him.

After I walked over and sat down, he immediately put his hand on my knee and said, "I'm glad you're here," while staring at me, which made me very uncomfortable.

"Why are you looking at me like that?" I asked.

"You're good to look at," he responded, then leaned over and kissed me on my lips.

I was shocked, confused, and needed a minute to think. This was all happening too fast.

When he grabbed my face and started to kiss me more passionately, I jumped up from the bed and said, "Slyy, what are you doing?"

He looked embarrassed and started apologizing. "I'm sorry, Music," he said, while standing up.

"Why did you kiss me? Why did I let you kiss me? Oh God, what have I've done?"

"When I see things I want, I don't hesitate to go after it. I don't know what I'm doing."

"I thought I wouldn't have to worry about things like this?"

"Music, I'm sorry."

"Don't let it happen again!" I yelled.

I felt disrespected and didn't care how big of a star he was. I was going to tell him how I felt.

Continuing to apologize, he said, "I hope nothing changes between us. You're family and Janice loves you. I wasn't thinking. Please forgive me."

I told him, "I forgive you."

He thought I was going to be like a groupie and do whatever he wanted me to do, but I had more respect for myself.

"I hope you can forget about what just happened," he said.

"I can as long as it doesn't happen again."

"Why did you let me kiss you?" Slyy asked with a grin on his face.

"I didn't let you. You caught me off guard."

"I think you liked it."

"I didn't!"

Garrett was knocking on the door, so Slyy got up and left without saying a word or looking back, while I sat on the bed still stunned.

~~~~~~~

It had been weeks since Slyy kissed me, and we were both acting like nothing ever happened. He never tried it again, so I felt comfortable around him and tried to forget about the incident.

Janice and I were around each other all the time, but she never found out what happened. By now, I was getting along much better with the dancers. At least they were pretending to be my friend.

As long as we had been traveling together, we had no choice but to talk to each other. They understood that they couldn't get me fired, so either they had to deal with me or they could go home. Things had definitely changed since our rehearsals days.

I stayed at Slyy and Janice's house in California whenever we had a day
~~~~~~~

off. Janice was so nice, spoiling me all the time. It was very cool talking to her because she always understood me. She gave me great advice about the business, men, and life.

Too bad she didn't really know what her man was doing. I wanted to tell her about Slyy kissing me, but I didn't want to hurt her feelings because she really loved him. So, as usual, I kept my mouth shut. Forgive, forget, and move on was what I started to get used to doing.

After being around Janice all the time, I realized she was a very jealous person. I never could understand how she could be rich and beautiful, yet so insecure. Sometimes she would drain me talking about other women in the business.

She was only happy and felt secure when she knew she had more money than other people and had on the most expensive outfit. She was struggling being around the dancers because we were all vibrant with great bodies.

Janice was in great shape and had the body of a twenty-year-old, but was used to being the only female on the tour where she got all the attention. Now she had to share the spotlight with four other women, which she was not happy about and struggled with regularly.

Even though I was friends with Janice, she was just as jealous of me as she was with the other dancers. She was no different from any other woman.

Slyy and Janice trusted me to stay at their house whenever they were away. I had my own bedroom and could stay there whenever I wanted to. They made me feel very comfortable and allowed me to drive their Range Rover or Mercedes, as well.

Janice even took me shopping to personalize my bedroom just the way I wanted it. Whenever I told my friends and family that I was staying at their house, they would get so excited.

This is when I remembered how famous they were. Being around them on tour so long, made them just like anyone else. They were no longer famous in my eyes; they were my family.

I tried to explain this to my friends, but they didn't understand. All they knew is that I was staying at Slyy and Janice's house and living the good life. So, I let them have their fantasies.

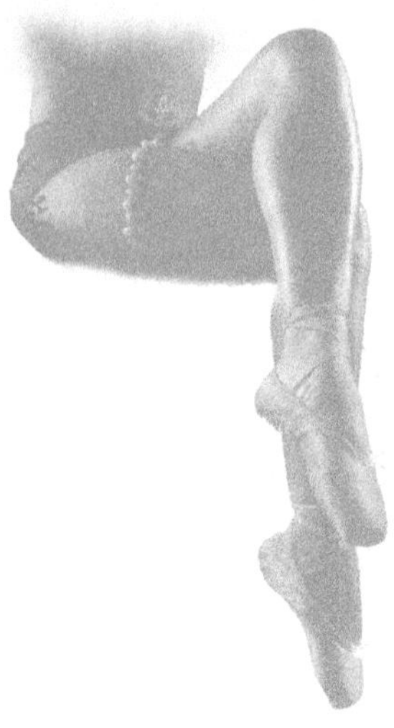

CHAPTER 20

We arrived in St. Louis hours before our show and went straight to the venue for sound check. As soon as we walked backstage, we noticed the same man that had been at our last two shows waiting in the backstage area.

We were in a different city every night, yet this man was constantly showing up. It was obvious we had a stalker.

"I love you, girls. Can I have your autograph?" the strange man asked us.

"Of course," we said reluctantly.

We signed autographs for him and then immediately went to our dressing room.

"Garrett, we need to talk to you," we said, while we grabbed his arm and pulled him into our dressing room.

"What's wrong with you guys?" Garrett asked.

"We think that man we just signed autographs for is stalking us. He has been in the last two cities."

"Well, that sounds like a stalker to me. I'll take care of it," Garrett said, as he left our dressing room and had security make the man leave.

The next day when we arrived in Indiana and walked into sound check, the same man was sitting in the front row. We stopped in our tracks and immediately told security.

"Who is the guy sitting in the front row?" security asked the promoter.

"He's a part of your tour," the promoter replied.

"He is not with our tour," security said.

"The guy has a tour pass and has been here since this morning," the promoter informed security.

By the time security finished talking to the promoter, the guy was gone. So, security went straight to Slyy's dressing room to tell him about the stalker.

"The dancers have a stalker and he's showing up in every city and they're scared," security told Slyy.

"Hire more security to look after them," Slyy said.

"I'll take care of it," security said.

"I told Garrett to take care of this a while ago. Let's keep them until the girls feel more comfortable," Slyy told security.

We were terrified, but tried to concentrate on getting ready for the show. Once the show started, we forgot about the stalker. During the show, we were in our dressing room changing for the next song and talking about how afraid we were of the spooky man. We felt safer having security right outside of our dressing room.

"I can't believe we have a stalker," Lisa said.

"That's what we get for being so beautiful," Ashley commented, as she continued getting ready for the show.

"I'm a little scared," Blanca blurted out.

Every time we came back to our dressing room for a quick wardrobe change for our next dance number, we noticed things were moved around and disappearing.

"Has anyone seen my shoes?" Blanca asked.

"I can't find my dress," I said out loud.

Ashley's pants were gone and Lisa was missing her makeup. We looked through the clothes hanging on the rack for the missing items, but didn't find them.

"Did that clothes rack just move?" Blanca asked.

"Yes, I just saw it move," I said fearfully.

"You guys are so paranoid," Ashley said.

Seeing that we were scared, Ashley played on that by laughing and saying, "What if the stalker is behind the rack of clothes?"

We started laughing at her, and Lisa told her to stop playing around.

Ashley stopped for a moment, then ran to the rack of clothes, pulled them back, and said, "Look I found the stalker!"

She was cracking up laughing until she noticed the look on our faces. We screamed and started running out the room. Ashley never looked at the rack, but when she saw us running, she started running with us. The security guard heard us screaming and opened the door. We almost knocked him down trying to get out.

We kept screaming, "The stalker is in the room!"

Security grabbed the stalker and removed him from the building. He was taken straight to jail. The stalker had been in our dressing room the entire time watching as we changed our clothes. He must have snuck in our dressing room and hid when we were on stage rehearsing at sound check.

After that incident, Slyy put a serious lockdown on our security. He made sure the promoters had a picture of everyone on our tour.

Blanca, Lisa, Ashley, and I were so afraid that security had to check our hotel room before we entered. We never used our real names when we checked into hotels. Slyy made sure everyone on the tour felt safe because he knew how it felt to be stalked.

It's going to take a long time for me to feel comfortable again. I'm going to always feel like someone is watching me. This was the part of show business that was not fun, but instead scary.

It's a lot of crazy people in the world, and for some reason, they are attracted to people in the entertainment business.

Life is never boring on tour; there is always something going on to keep me on my toes.

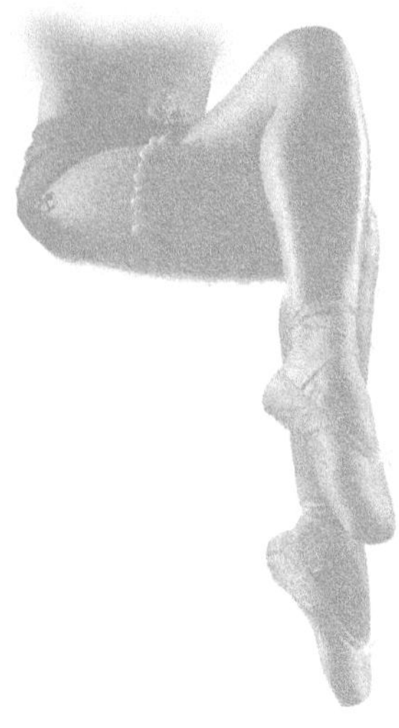

CHAPTER 21

"Hey, Bubba," we said, while getting on the bus to head to the next city.

Bubba had worked with Slyy for years and was always personally requested. Usually, the bus company would send any driver available, but Slyy really liked him and always used him as his personal driver. Bubba was so loyal to Slyy that he would leave jobs to drive for him.

Bubba was very funny and always wore blue jean overalls and old t-shirts. His white hair, long white beard, and big stomach made him look like Santa Claus. He sang songs while driving and entertained us by telling jokes.

We made sure he was well taken care of because he was part of our family. Slyy even allowed him to watch all the shows and stay at the same five-star hotels we did. This was not normal for drivers, who were usually treated badly and stayed at low-budget hotels.

After five hours on the bus, we stopped at a truck stop so Bubba could gas up the bus.

"If you want to get some snacks, be back on the bus in ten minutes," Garrett announced.

I wasn't hungry, but I got off the bus to stretch my legs. With Slyy, Janice, and the dancers joining me, we stood in front of the bus laughing and talking.

"Can I talk to you in private?" Bubba asked Slyy.

"Sure," Slyy said, as he took only a few steps away from us.

By the look on Bubba's face, it was not the privacy that he wanted.

"I was wondering if I could get a raise," Bubba asked.

"Let me talk to my accountant and get back to you," Slyy responded.

I knew that meant he was not going to get a raise and he was brushing him off.

"No problem," Bubba said.

~~~~~~~

A month later, Bubba asked Slyy again at one of our sound checks for a raise. Slyy was upset because Bubba wouldn't let it go.

"I'm not giving out any raises during this tour," Slyy finally told him.

"I deserve a raise," Bubba said raising his voice.

"We can discuss your raise for the next tour," Slyy said angrily.

"I want a raise now!" Bubba shouted.

"No!" Slyy shouted back.

"You have the money to pay me. Why are you being so cheap?" Bubba said.

"I said no! Now stop asking me!" Slyy replied loudly.

"I have been loyal to you and deserve a raise," Bubba said.

"I don't want to talk about this anymore. If you don't like what you're getting paid, then leave!" Slyy yelled.

They were having a shouting match on stage in the middle of sound check, while everyone was watching and listening. Bubba walked away without saying anything.

As Bubba dropped us off at the hotel after the show, he didn't seem to care that he was not getting a raise and was acting like his normal self.
~~~~~~~

The next day, we were in the hotel lobby waiting on Bubba to take us to sound check. Garrett kept looking outside waiting for the tour bus to pull up, as he continued to call Bubba but got no response.

After we were thirty minutes late for sound check, Garrett called a taxi for everyone, including Slyy, and we were on our way.

We never heard from Bubba again, and we missed our show the next day because we did not have transportation. Bubba stole the bus with all of our personal belongings inside.

Slyy had his people searching for Bubba, but he had disappeared. We never got our personal belongings back; however, we did receive a check for the missing items from the bus company. We also received a new bus and new driver to finish the tour.

~~~~~~~

A few weeks later, in the middle of our show, I looked over and noticed that one of the background singers was missing. I continued dancing until Garrett waved his hands in the air trying to get our attention, while security escorted Janice away from the side of the stage.

Ashley danced around Slyy and got him to look in Garrett's direction. Since he continued to sing and didn't respond to him, we kept dancing. By now, all of the background singers had left the stage. Then we saw Garrett and the promoter trying to pull the band members off the stage, but they wouldn't leave.

Finally, the promoter and Garrett ran on stage, yelling, "Get off the stage now!"

Garrett grabbed Slyy by the arm and pulled him towards the exit, while the promoter snatched the microphone from Slyy and said, "There's a bomb in the building! Please leave now!"

Immediately, pandemonium broke out. We ran out of the venue and kept running until we saw our tour bus parked next to the building. We were falling down and screaming trying to get on the bus, but we couldn't find the driver.
~~~~~~~

It made no sense to be on the bus that was so close to the building, but we were just happy to be out.

Nervous, I cried and kept asking, “What’s going on?”

“Oh my God!” Blanca said, shaking.

“I’m trying to find out as much information as I can. I need to make sure everyone is out of the building,” Garrett said nervously, while Slyy sat in utter shock.

A few minutes later, the promoter came on the bus and announced that it was a false alarm.

“Whew!” Slyy said, as he wiped the sweat from his forehead.

“Can I talk to you in private?” The promoter asked Slyy.

They went in the room on the back of the bus, and Janice followed them. We ran to the back with our ears pressed against the door to listen.

“What the hell just happened?” Slyy asked franticly as soon as he closed the door.

“The building received a call from a person saying there was a bomb in the building,” the promoter explained.

“Who the hell would do something like this?” Slyy asked.

“We just received another call from the same person who told us to relay a message to you,” the promoter said, fearful.

“What kind of message?” Slyy inquired suspiciously.

“He said you should have paid,” the promoter said, as he looked directly into Slyy’s eyes.

“I should have paid what?” Slyy asked.

“Do you know this person?” The promoter asked curiously.

“No! I don’t know who it could be. I don’t owe anyone,” Slyy said puzzled.

Janice was so terrified that she remained quiet.

“The police are waiting to talk to you in your dressing room,” the promoter said, as he escorted Slyy out of the room.

We ran from the door terrified after hearing their conversation.

When they came out of the room, Blanca immediately said, “I want to go home.”

“It was a false alarm. You can relax now,” Slyy said, trying to appear calm.

Looking at Janice facial expression, we knew this was nothing to relax about, and we insisted that he cancel the second show.

Slyy became very angry. “I’m not going to lose any more money. I have to refund everyone’s money from the first show.”

I kept crying, Blanca kept shaking, and everyone else put their heads down. We were not looking forward to doing a second show in the same building.

“Get yourselves together and be ready to go on stage in a couple of hours!” Slyy said, then walked off the bus and slammed the door.

“Slyy wouldn’t put us in danger. If he’s comfortable with doing the second show, you should be, too,” Janice told everyone.

“We heard what they were talking about in the room, and I’m scared,” I said.

“The show must go on,” Janice replied.

Money drives people, and even if it meant our safety, we had to suck it up and prepare for the second show, which ended up being uncomfortable and stressful.

During the show, we kept glancing to the side of the stage because we didn’t want to miss our signal to leave. Thankfully, there were no more bomb threats.

From that show forward, at least once a month, we had a bomb threat and had to evacuate the building in the middle of our shows. We began to get used to the threats and were no longer afraid, but instead, we started expecting them.

We stopped leaving the stage and created a special cue in the show to deal with the threats. Whenever the band got a signal from the promoter about another bomb threat, the band made a loud explosion sound and told the audience that it was time for an intermission.

The audience evacuated the building and was given a raffle ticket on their way out. Once the show continued, Slyy selected a raffle ticket and gave away a thousand dollars to the winner. Slyy never told the audience there was a bomb threat, but he knew he couldn't continue giving his personal money away.

When word got out that Slyy's intermission for his shows was actually an evacuation for a bomb threat, the ticket sells started declining. It was all over the news and people were scared to attend the shows.

In the middle of our show one night, Slyy said into the microphone "I'm not scared, and whoever keeps making these bomb threats needs to talk to me personally. Stop being a coward!"

The next day, another call was made with a personal message to Slyy. The caller said, "You should have given me a raise." From that message, Slyy knew it was Bubba, our old bus driver, making all the bomb threats. Bubba's plan had worked because Slyy lost money from the shows that were cancelled.

After the police got involved, Bubba was finally located and arrested, but he was quickly released because they didn't have proof it was him making the threats. So, he was a free man and could continue to scare the hell out of us.

I didn't know how much longer I could deal with it. I loved dancing, but my life is more important.

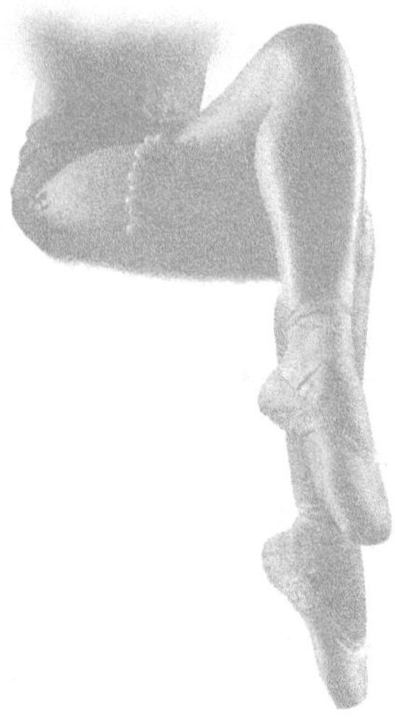

CHAPTER 22

We arrived in Baltimore and checked into the hotel, while still trying to forget about Bubba and his bomb threats. As soon as I got in the room, I called my cousin Sydney to give her an update on what was going on.

Two hours later, there was a loud knock at my door that frightened me. I quickly got off the telephone and went straight to the door to look out the peephole. It was Janice.

After I opened the door, she pushed me to the side and walked in. She looked in the bathroom, then opened the closet and looked inside. I was still standing at the door watching her.

"What are you looking for, Janice?"

She didn't respond. Instead, she continued looking around my room.

I slammed the door and said very sternly, "What are you doing?"

She suddenly stopped.

I walked over to her and said, "What's up?"

"Have you seen Slyy?" Janice asked.

"No, and he wouldn't be in my closet if I had seen him!"

Janice had a weird, deranged look on her face, and her expression worried me.

She then snapped out of whatever crazy movie scene she was in and jokingly said, "Girl, I haven't been able to contact Slyy. I know he's up to something."

"Why would you think he was in my room?"

"I don't know, Music. He's driving me crazy."

"You need to relax!" I said, irritated.

"The wedding plans have me so preoccupied; we hardly ever spend time together. Now that he's drinking again, I can't keep up with him. When he drinks, he becomes a different person, and I can't trust him," Janice told me.

"Just relax. You just have a lot going on. Maybe you can get him back in rehab."

"I guess I'm getting nervous. You know how women are. We always think our man is cheating on us," she replied, hoping that Slyy was faithful.

I didn't comment because I knew Slyy was a dirty dog.

"Do you think he's cheating with anyone on the tour?" Janice asked me.

My eyes opened wide. I shrugged my shoulders and replied, "I don't think so."

I really wanted to say *yes, he's cheating because he kissed me,* but I couldn't tell her because she looked so pitiful.

"Can you keep an eye on Slyy and make sure he's not cheating?" Janice said.

She knew he was very flirtatious, and she couldn't control him.

"Why are you with him if you think he's cheating on you?"

"I have never caught him with anyone, but my intuition tells me he's doing something wrong."

"You can have any man you want. Why do you deal with him?"

"I love him."

"Maybe you should go with your intuition. If you think something is going on, it probably is," I told her.

"When a woman has an intuition about a man cheating, it's usually true," she responded.

"Well, I always follow my first mind," I said.

"Can you just keep an eye on him?" Janice asked, frustrated.

"Okay," I said hesitantly, seeing the sadness in her eyes.

I knew Slyy was a cheater, but I wasn't sure if I could tell her that he had tried to cheat with me.

After every show, we got invited to the hottest club in town. Since we had started going to clubs, I saw exactly what Janice told me about Slyy.

When he got drunk, he became a different person. He was very loud, said nasty things to women, and would take his sunglasses off so you could see the crazy look in his glazed eyes.

It was difficult being around him in a drunken stupor. The other dancers and band members didn't mind because that meant free drinks and money for everyone. When intoxicated, Slyy was very free with his money, giving it to us all night long. We could get anything we wanted from him when he was drunk.

The dancers especially knew how to work him because they were females. All they had to do was dress sexy, rub up against him and say nice things, and he would give them anything they asked for. It was sad watching everyone take advantage of him, although I did benefit from it, too.

Ever since I told Janice I would keep an eye on Slyy, she has constantly asked me what he was doing, where he was, and who he was with. She also forced me to go out with him to parties.

I went out after the shows with Slyy, but sometimes, I didn't feel like going and just wanted to go back to my hotel room and relax.

Slyy would get upset when I tried to stop him from drinking. He cursed me out so badly one night in front of everyone that I never tried to stop him again.

Whenever Janice was on the road with us, she would accuse every woman, including me, of messing around with Slyy. She was extremely jealous, and Slyy was partially to blame for her insecurities. She was rubbing everyone the wrong way, and we couldn't deal with her new personality.

When everyone started complaining to Slyy about Janice's behavior, he decided to ask her to leave the tour. He told her that she could focus on the wedding plans while she was off the road.

Janice wasn't happy to leave the tour, but knew she had a huge wedding to plan and needed to be home. So, she left without a big fight.

Slyy wanted her off the tour just as much as everyone else because she stopped him from having fun. We felt like we were walking on eggshells when she was around.

I realized celebrities are no different than regular people. They get jealous, do crazy things, and act childish like the rest of us.

CHAPTER 23

"Hello, bitches!" Queen said, as we walked into rehearsals.

We were scheduled to perform on a televised awards show in Los Angeles, and Slyy hired ten new dancers to make the show more elaborate. Being face-to-face with Queen again brought back horrible memories.

During rehearsals, Queen made sure Lisa, Ashley, Blanca, and I was front and center, and didn't get lost on stage with the new dancers, who we knew would try to get a permanent job with Slyy. We were nervous because we knew we could be replaced.

The next day after rehearsals, Blanca, Ashley, Lisa, and I spent the entire day getting ready for the awards show. We seemed to be getting along great and were tolerating each other.

We pampered ourselves by getting manicures, pedicures, massages, and facials. Afterwards, we went shopping for clothes so we would stand out in the crowd.

I was tired from all the shopping we did and happy to be back in my hotel room to unwind. I dropped my bags on the floor, ordered room service, and took a hot shower.

Not long after I got out of the shower, there was a knock on my door. I was hungry and hoping it was room service. When I opened the door, Garrett quickly pushed Slyy into my room. It was obvious he was sloppy drunk.

I didn't feel like being bothered. I was tired and wanted to relax. Garrett helped Slyy sit down on the bed.

"What's wrong with him?" I asked Garrett, while watching as Slyy slurred his words and struggled to sit up straight.

"He went out drinking with some friends, and I wasn't there to watch him," Garrett replied disappointedly.

"Oh Lord! You know how he gets when he's drunk," I said.

Garrett had been around Slyy before he became famous, and he always watched his back. He was like an older brother to him and the only person Slyy trusted. Slyy paid him a six-figure salary for his services and loyalty.

Garrett was famous in his own eyes and living the American dream. He was popular, rich with power, and was never going to leave Slyy. This was as close as he would get to being famous without having any talent.

Garrett said, "I'm going to go and get some coffee for him."

"I ordered room service and they should be here shortly," I informed Garrett.

"I will stop them in the hallway. Don't let anyone in this room."

"Why did you bring him to my room?" I asked.

"I can't trust anyone else. Keep an eye on him until I get back," Garrett said, then left out of the room.

I didn't feel like being his babysitter, but I tried to help him by putting a wet towel on his head.

"Stop!" he yelled, as he hit the towel out of my hand and started vomiting all over the floor.

He was crying and talking foolish. I couldn't understand what he was saying and was hoping Garrett would return soon. I had never seen him like this before, and it frightened me.

"I love you, Music," Slyy said, slurring his words.

"You're drunk and need to stop talking," I told him.

"Did you hear what I said? I want you," Slyy said.

"Garrett will be back soon with the coffee. Don't talk."

I knew he didn't know what he was saying, and I wanted him to be quiet. I got a bottle of water out of the mini bar, and when I went to hand it to him he knocked the water out of my hand and grabbed my wrist.

"Stop! You're hurting me!" I screamed.

"I'm not trying to hurt you," he said.

"Let go!" I yelled.

"Make love to me!" He demanded.

"You're drunk and talking crazy," I said.

"Do you love me?" He asked, while squeezing my wrist harder.

"Yes, I love you. Please let go!" I screamed in pain. I would say anything to make him stop.

"Do you want me?" Slyy asked, as he looked into my eyes.

"No. We're family, remember?" I replied.

Becoming very upset, he pushed me down on the bed and got on top me while pinning my wrist down.

"Why don't you want me?" He asked.

"Stop!" I cried.

"Don't tell me to stop. Do you know who I am?" Slyy said, as he slapped me.

I continued crying while trying to fight him off.

"I'm sick of you being Miss Goody Two Shoes. I want you, and I'm going to have you," he said.

"Stop, Slyy!" I yelled, as he grabbed my t-shirt and ripped it off. "No! Get off of me!" I screamed right before he covered my mouth with his hand.

When I tried to bite his hand, he slapped me again. Then he tried to take my shorts off while he was trying to kiss me. I was grossed out by the smell of vomit on his breath.

We were wrestling on the bed, and he grabbed my hair and punched me in my ribs. I curled up in a fetal position, crying.

"Why are you doing this to me?" I asked.

My question still didn't stop him. He grabbed both of my hands and started bending them backwards.

"Never tell me no!" He said.

I started screaming again. I thought for sure he would break my wrists. Hearing a knock at the door, I prayed it was Garrett. Slyy acted like he didn't hear anything.

All of a sudden, the knocking stopped. Slyy continued hitting me while trying to take my clothes off. I fought back by kicking, biting, and scratching, but this didn't stop him. He was too strong and overpowered me.

I was in so much pain I couldn't fight anymore. First he snatched off my shorts and panties. Then he started choking me while forcefully entering me. I stopped fighting back, hoping he would stop.

He was going to have sex with me, and there was nothing I could do about it. Once he finished raping me, he got up and zipped his pants, while I laid there crying.

"I didn't have to do this if you would have given me what I wanted. If you tell anyone about this, I will kill you," Slyy said, looking at me lying on the bed.

I was too fearful to say anything.

"I own you and will have you anytime I want," he added.

While Slyy was talking to me, the hotel security rushed into the room with Garrett. Slyy's shirt was ripped and his arms were bleeding from me scratching him.

Garrett looked at Slyy and then at me in the bed before rushing the security to the door.

"Everything's okay in here," he told them.

When security showed no signs of leaving, Garrett walked over to me, grabbed my arm tightly, and said, "Tell them you're okay,"

He had the same crazy look in his eyes that Slyy had. I wanted to yell to the security guard to help me, but he was squeezing my arm tightly and I was terrified.

"I'm fine," I softly said.

"She's fine," Garrett turned around and told them.

The security guards took a long look at me and knew something was wrong, but since it was Slyy, they didn't do anything. Before they left the room, Garrett handed them some hush money while giving them a handshake.

Once they were gone, Garrett took Slyy into the bathroom, and I could hear them talking. I tried to get up off the bed to leave the room, but I couldn't move. I only managed to sit up on the side of the bed.

When they came out of the bathroom, Garrett walked over to me and said, "I know you're not going to mention this to anyone, right?"

I looked at Garrett and didn't say a word as the tears continued running down my face.

"He's drunk," Garrett said, trying to apologize for Slyy.

I looked at Garrett in disbelief that he would make an excuse for him.

"He raped me!" I told Garrett.

Before I could get another word out, Garret slapped me so hard I flew over the bed and landed on the floor.

"Don't ever let me hear you say that again! If he had sex with you, it's because you wanted him to, and if he beat you, then I guess you deserved it. If I ever hear you saying anything about this to anyone, I will make your life a living hell."

I laid on the floor in agony.

"I will call a doctor and have him come over to check you out. I don't need you going to the hospital making a big stink about this and alerting the police. This needs to be kept confidential. And don't think about leaving this tour, because I need to keep an eye on you."

I listened to my instructions, while Slyy stood at the door realizing how badly I was injured. Garrett took out his cell phone and dialed a number.

"A friend of mine needs help because her boyfriend beat her up. Are you available now?" Garrett said. He then gave the person the address and room number. "Someone will be here in about an hour. I will leave the door open for them. Don't talk to them. Just let them take care of you. If they have any questions, they can contact me."

Garrett came on the side of the bed where I was still lying on the floor and helped me back on the bed. He looked shocked after seeing the bruises all over my body, and then he looked at Slyy.

"Don't leave this room. Wait for the doctors to come. Do you understand?" Garrett asked.

"Yes," I responded.

"Let's get out of here! You don't need to be seen anywhere around this room," Garrett told Slyy.

They left me in pain, and less than an hour later, the doctor showed up with an assistant. They immediately started working on me. When they asked where it hurt, I pointed to my injuries.

The doctor gave me a shot in my arm, while the assistant put ice packs around my wrists and listened to my heartbeat. They made me take some medicine, saying it would make me feel better. I didn't even ask what type of medicine I was taking. I just wanted the pain to go away.

"I need you to take this morning-after pill to make sure you're not pregnant," the assistant told me.

They definitely had done this before and were used to treating Slyy's victims. They worked on me for about two hours and then gave me another shot in both of my wrists.

"Your wrists will feel better in a couple of hours," I was told, but my wrists were hurting so badly that I didn't believe them.

The doctor then said, “This medicine will make you sleepy. We’ll be back in the morning to check on you. What time is sound check for the awards show?”

“Two o’clock. Are my ribs broken?” I asked.

“No,” he answered.

“Will I be able to dance at the show tomorrow?”

“You’ll be just like new,” he assured me.

He looked at me strange while answering my questions, probably because I wasn’t following instructions by not talking to them. He wasn’t supposed to talk to me either, but I needed to know what kind of condition I was in.

“Get some rest and we’ll see you tomorrow,” he said, then they gathered all their belongings and left.

I tried to fight the sleep, but I gave in and was knocked out until the next morning.

The next day, I woke up starring at the ceiling, praying that everything that happened last night was just a really bad dream. I got up expecting to be just as sore as I was last night, but I actually felt great. It was a miracle.

The doctor told me to take the medicine he left on the nightstand immediately when I woke up and then wait thirty minutes before I started moving around. What did they give me and how was I able to function? A part of me wanted to know, and another part of me didn’t care as long as I felt better.

I contemplated telling my family what happened, but then kept seeing Slyy and Garrett’s face while they threatened me if I told anyone. I lay in bed thinking about what I should do and wondering if Slyy had done this to any of the other dancers.

I wanted to go home, but I had worked so hard to be here and deserved this opportunity. I needed something to keep me going. I didn’t know what I was going to do, but I did know I had a show in a few hours and needed to be ready.

My family and friends told me I had made it dancing for Slyy. They always expressed how proud they were of me and to keep doing what I was doing. I kept hearing them over and over in my head, and I didn't want to disappoint them. I felt so much pressure to continue dancing.

I couldn't trust anyone to tell them what happened. I remember Garrett telling me when I first started dancing with Slyy to learn how to keep a secret and to keep my mouth shut. So, I would keep dancing and be quiet until I could figure out a plan.

I was still thinking about the crazy look on Slyy's face, which gave me chills. The telephone rang and it was Garrett. He wanted to make sure I continued to be petrified.

"How are you doing? Are you able to dance?" Garrett asked nicely.

"Yes, I'm ready," I said.

"Don't be stupid and start running your mouth," he warned.

"I won't say anything. I know how to keep secrets."

"Good. Slyy worked too hard to have someone destroy his career over something like this."

I knew better than to say anything. My face was still stinging from Garrett slapping me across the bed, and he wanted to make sure I would remember not to say the word "rape" again.

I stayed quiet while Garrett talked. What scared me the most was that he never raised his voice. He remained calm the whole time he reiterated how he would make my life a living hell if I said anything or left the tour.

After talking to Garrett, I became upset with him threatening me and knew I didn't have to take it. Getting some courage, I decided to call my friend who was a police officer. I figured he could explain my rights and give me some direction on what to do.

I took a deep breath and slowly dialed his number. After he answered on the second ring, we started catching up with each other's lives. He was doing very well and had just moved into a new house.

"How's life on the road?" He asked me.

At that very moment, I started crying and became very nervous.

"Music, what's wrong?"

I almost didn't tell him, but I felt that he was definitely going to step in and do something. So, I took a deep breath and told him about the night Slyy beat and raped me. He listened in shock, but was no help.

He was star-struck and more interested in information about Slyy, what entertainers I met, what city we were touring in, and could he get some free tickets to the show. He wanted some gossip, and I needed some help.

"I thought you were going to help me. You're turning your cheek and acting like nothing happened because of who he is. I needed your help!" I said as I hung up the telephone,

I hoped he didn't tell anyone, but I knew he would tell everyone this juicy gossip. The only good thing is he was not in the entertainment business, so whomever he told it would not get back to Slyy or Garrett.

Crazy things were always happening in the entertainment business, and if you were just a dancer, you were not going to get any help or respect. Dancers were on the bottom of the list.

I was strong, so I kept dealing with the situation and praying. I knew the day would come when I could stand on my own and walk away. I had already taken a stand by calling my friend and asking for help, even though he didn't give me any.

I was on my own to deal with it, but the first thing I needed to focus on was getting through the show. I lay down and waited for the doctor to arrive, hoping I would be able to dance.

CHAPTER 24

Slyy was so nervous about this show. He wanted everyone ready and waiting downstairs an hour before our call time, so we would not be late.

I checked around my room and made sure I had everything. Then I did a few dance moves to confirm I wasn't going to be in any pain. I was good, although my wrists were still aching.

The doctor gave me wrist braces to wear while I was in the room, but instructed me to take them off before I left.

When I tried to remove them, my wrists felt worse. So, I put them back on until I was ready to walk out the door. I took more of the medicine and hoped my wrists would feel better.

Rushing, I grabbed my belongings and went to the lobby to wait. Everyone was coming down, ready and excited. I tried to act like everything was normal, but I was messed up inside.

I looked at the other dancers while they were heading towards the lobby and wondered if Slyy had done this to them. Blanca had been dancing with him the longest, and maybe that's why she'd been there so long.

I smiled at everyone and tried to act like nothing was wrong, but tears started rolling down my cheek because my body was still in pain. Not wanting anyone to think something was wrong, I wiped them away quickly. The medicine I took made my ribs feel better, but it didn't help my wrists much.

Blanca walked over to me and asked, "What's wrong with your wrists?"

I had totally forgotten to take the braces off before I left the room. By this time, everyone was asking me what happened. Garrett walked over to me right away.

"I have carpal tunnel in my wrists and have to wear the braces sometimes. I forgot to take them off," I said.

Blanca looked at me very strangely, as if she knew I was lying, but it seemed like everyone else believed the lie. Garrett never said a word. He just rolled his eyes and walked away.

Slyy arrived in the hotel lobby and personally spoke to everyone. He then walked over to me, gave me a hug as usual, and said, "Hello." The only difference was this time he whispered in my ear, "Don't fuck with me."

I looked at him and tried to keep a smile on my face, while my teeth were chattering out of fear. I was so shook up that I walked out of the hotel and got in the van quickly. No one suspected anything, and Garrett made sure he kept an eye on me the whole time.

Although I was in pain during the show and tears ran down my face, the show was amazing. It was hard for me to enjoy it because my body ached. I was used to dancing with injuries, but mentally and emotionally, I was devastated.

After the show, Garrett said, "Slyy wants to talk to you in his dressing room."

I went to his dressing room trembling with fear.

"Come in and close the door," Slyy instructed me.

I closed the door behind me and started shaking uncontrollably.

"Relax. I'm not going to hurt you," Slyy said with a smile, while drinking a shot of Hennessy.

Still trembling, I sat down next to him. I was never going to be able to relax around him because I didn't know him anymore. I avoided looking at him for fear that I would see that deranged look he had in his eyes last night.

He grabbed my wrists and I jumped. My wrists were still in pain, and I thought he was going to finish the job and break them.

"I'm sorry about last night," he said, while rubbing my wrists. "How are you doing, baby?"

"I'm fine," I replied.

"Did you tell anyone what happened?" he asked, as he rubbed my wrists harder.

"No!" I blurted out.

"That's a good girl. Can you forgive me?"

"Yes," I said quietly, while looking down at the floor.

"I will never hurt you again. I love you, Music," he stated, as he took another sip of his drink.

I never responded.

"You felt good last night, and now I need to have you all the time," he said, as he caressed my thighs.

"No! I can't do that."

Before I could finish my sentence, he slapped me and I went flying to the floor.

"I told you never to tell me no," Slyy said, as he stood over me.

Holding my face, I looked up at him and asked, "Why are you doing this to me?"

He hit me again. "I always get what I want and right now, I want you."

When he helped me up and started rubbing my face, I knew then he needed serious help and I wanted to get away from him.

"Make sure you keep it hot for me."

I looked at him, wanting to punch him in his mouth, but I just didn't have the nerve to do it.

"You can leave now," Slyy said, as he gestured with his hand for me to get out.

Without any hesitation, I left swiftly.

I had never been beaten by a man, and when Slyy hit me, it did something mentally to me. I was messed up and lost all my control.

I'm sure if I told anyone what he was doing to me, they would ask why did I stay and allow him to continue to do this. But, it's always easy to make a comment when you're not the one living in horror.

I used to always say if a man hit me, I would leave. I never could understand how a woman could stay with a man that beat her. Now I did, and I didn't know why I couldn't leave. I guess my thoughts were the same as every battered woman.

I took him very seriously about killing me. When you have money and fame, you can do anything you want and get away with it. I once was a strong woman, but now I felt stripped of my strength.

The entertainment business could be best compared to a drug. You will do anything to get that first high, and once you get it, you want to keep experiencing that feeling. You keep running after it. The money you received was also like a drug. It's what kept most people in the business. The money was definitely what kept me in the business so long.

People in the business are not happy because there are ups and downs, but because you love the fame and money, it makes you endure unless you are forced to leave.

CHAPTER 25

A week later after my horrible experience with Slyy and Garrett, I ran into Que backstage at one of our shows. It had been a long time since I danced for Destruction's music video, and I was happy to see him. Que went solo when his group broke up, and he ended up being very successful.

"Why didn't you tell me that you were the opening act for Slyy's show tonight?" I asked Que, excited.

"I wanted to surprise you," he said, giving me a big hug and kiss on my cheek.

"You definitely surprised me," I replied, smiling.

"My album just went platinum, and I'm working on my second one," he announced proudly.

"Congratulations! I'm so happy for you," I responded, giving him another hug.

"I've been checking you out and you look fine as hell on stage," Que said, as he stroked my hair.

"Thanks," I said.

"Damn, Music, I didn't know you looked so good. You can't be my little sister anymore."

"Why?"

"Because I might want to hook up with you," Que said with a smile.

Que was such a flirt, but he knew we were strictly platonic friends. He was a big brother to me, which was as far as it had ever gone.

"You've got to dance on my next tour."

"I'll be there."

"By the time Slyy's tour is over, I'll be starting rehearsal for my tour. The timing is perfect."

"We will finally work together. I can't wait to get started," I said.

"Neither one of our telephone numbers have changed in years, so we have no excuse for not keeping in contact," Que said.

"You're right. I'll do better."

"I would love to have Slyy on my next album. Can you introduce me to him?" Que asked.

"I'll take you to his dressing room now," I said.

Slyy knew exactly who Que was, and he was interested in working with him, also. Anyone who was hot on the scene and blazing the charts, Slyy wanted to be connected with them.

Que didn't waste any time telling Slyy how much he respected him and always dreamed of working with him. Slyy told him that he loved his work and thought he was very talented.

They exchanged telephone numbers and started planning their next move together. Slyy even invited Que to travel with us to the next couple of cities. He knew Que's reputation in the business of being a ladies' man, so he wanted to hang out with him. They kept talking and didn't even notice me leaving.

When Que invited Slyy on stage during his performance, the crowd went wild. They sang Que's hit song together, and afterward, Que announced that they would be working together on his next album. The crowd stood on their feet, clapping and screaming. This was Que and Slyy's confirmation that their partnering together would be successful.

~~~~~~~

A month had past and Que was coming on the road with us every chance he got. He enjoyed hanging around Slyy and getting the inside scoop of the business.

Slyy continued to rape and beat me anytime he wanted to. I stopped fighting back because it was getting hard to cover up the bruises on my body. I never told anyone about the rapes. Instead, I became the best actress, pretending like nothing was going on. Slyy continued to control me by keeping me around him all the time.

Since Que was on the road with us occasionally, I wanted to tell him what was going on, but decided not to. I knew if I told Que, he would be upset and want to confront Slyy. I didn't want him to miss out on his opportunity for them to work together. So, I kept it moving and kept my mouth shut.

Because I was around Slyy all the time, the dancers and band members started gossiping, telling everyone that we were sleeping together. Some were saying they couldn't believe I would date him when I was friends with Janice. They didn't know he forced me to be around him and that I didn't have a choice.

If they only knew he was abusing me on a regular basis, they would understand my situation and know I wasn't that type of person. I started to think the road would make me stronger or kill me slowly, and I felt like I was dying.

After Blanca called Janice to tell her about the rumors, Janice came back on the road immediately. When she returned, she started giving me nasty looks and making smart remarks.

I was tempted to tell her what was really going on, but the negative spotlight was on me and I knew no one would believe a word I said.

I should have stopped everything from the beginning by saying something to somebody. Now things were out of control, and I didn't know how to stop it. I was at my breaking point and couldn't take the abuse from Slyy anymore. So, I decided to take a stand and fight back.
~~~~~~~

Ever since Janice was back on the road with us, I was able to make certain comments to Slyy without him knocking me upside my head. I had gotten very bold and would give him a piece of my mind every chance I got. He wasn't coming to my room as much because Janice was around.

I started fighting back and this started slowing down his visits. I told him I was not taking it anymore and would not open my door for him. I don't know where all the courage came from, but I had to take advantage of it.

I was happy Janice was on the road with us because her presence made Slyy act differently and was the reason why he stopped visiting my room.

CHAPTER 26

Headed to the next city on the tour, we was about to watch a movie on the bus when Slyy made an announcement. "I fired Lisa."

"Why?" Ashley asked.

"Because she took another job and would have to miss one of my shows. There are no days off on my tour," Slyy said.

Lisa had an opportunity to dance with another platinum artist, and this was the job she had been waiting for her entire dance career. I was shocked that he would fire her during the tour.

"I hired another dancer to replace her and finish the rest of the tour," he informed us.

No one said a word because we were so surprised.

"You guys will have a brief rehearsal with the new dancer at sound check tomorrow. Teach her the routines to get her ready for the European tour," he said.

We had all become closer and were sad to see Lisa leave. We didn't know what to expect from the new dancer and was afraid we wouldn't get along with her.

The next day at sound check, we couldn't wait to meet the new dancer. In the middle of rehearsal, she walked on stage and my mouth fell to the floor. It was Raven.

I couldn't believe Slyy hired Raven to replace Lisa. This was a bombshell. I didn't know if I was happy or upset to see her. We hadn't spoken since I started dancing for Slyy.

I couldn't seem to forget how crazy she was acting the last time we danced together. She had a major attitude and was on an ego trip.

Raven had a funny look on her face when she saw me. I was wondering why she didn't call and tell me that she was hired to dance for Slyy. She knew I was dancing for him, and I would have loved to have known she was coming.

Raven knew one of Slyy's band members, who introduced her to him a few months prior. Raven became friends with Slyy and was waiting for her spot on his tour. Once Slyy fired Lisa, the job was hers.

"This is Raven, the new dancer. Teach her as much as you can before the show tonight," Garrett said.

"What's up?" Raven said, greeting everyone.

Blanca and Ashley gave her the same attitude they gave me when I first met them. They were not friendly at all.

"Hey you," I said, while giving her a hug and trying to be friendly.

"Hey, Music," Raven responded with a smirk on her face.

"Why didn't you tell me that we would be working together?" I asked.

"I just found out myself. Now we're both working for Slyy."

"That's great!" I replied, trying to sound excited.

"Yes, it is," Raven said sarcastically.

The way Raven was looking at me, I knew she had not changed her ways and could not be trusted.

"Do you guys know each other?" Blanca asked.

"We used to dance together," I replied.

Raven interrupted and said, "We're old friends."

"That's good to know, because I don't feel like getting to know a stranger," Ashley responded with an attitude.

"Now that we know each other, let's get started," Blanca said.

Raven caught on to the routines quickly, which made Blanca happy. Because I knew Raven had a problem with me giving her directions, I never said a word and allowed Blanca and Ashley to teach her the choreography.

"What's going on with you guys?" Blanca asked after noticing that Raven and I were not talking.

"Nothing," I answered nonchalantly.

"You guys are not acting like friends," Blanca said.

I didn't want to get into the problems Raven and I were having, but Blanca wasn't going to let it go.

"Raven and I have been friends since we were kids, but the last time we danced together, she had a problem with me giving her direction. She wants to be in charge and in the spotlight," I said.

"We all want to be in the spotlight," Blanca said, interrupting.

"I don't have a problem with that because there's room for everyone, but I didn't think she would treat me differently. She's a different person to me, and I don't know her anymore," I said.

"Wow, I'm sorry to hear that. That happens in this business. She seems really cool, though," Blanca stated.

"She was very cool. Maybe she's back to normal."

It was breaking my heart that I couldn't be excited about dancing with Raven because this was the dream we had all our lives. I never thought we wouldn't be experiencing it together.

"You guys have one hour before the show starts. You need to start getting ready," Garrett announced.

In the dressing room, Raven made it a point not to show me any attention as she continued to talk to Blanca and Ashley. After being in the business so long, I had developed thick skin, so this didn't bother me. I tried to ignore Raven and continued getting ready for the show.

Raven was struggling because she wanted to dance in the show that night, but Slyy wanted her to wait until we started the overseas tour. So, she watched from the side of the stage.

Raven started hanging out with the band members and tried hard to be Blanca and Ashley's new best friend. She hung out with Slyy daily and made sure everyone knew she was the head bitch in charge. Once again, Janice was not on the road with us, and Raven took advantage of that.

Raven didn't waste any time trying to turn everyone against me by spreading rumors. She wanted me out of the picture and off the tour fast. She told the band members that I was jealous of her and didn't tell her that Slyy was looking for a new dancer.

Raven was constantly telling everyone this lie, and Blanca and Ashley became bothered by it. Soon, I started getting strange looks from everyone.

"I think you should know that Raven is spreading rumors about you," Blanca informed me.

"What rumor?" I asked, rather stunned.

"She's telling everyone you're jealous of her and didn't tell her that Slyy was looking for a new dancer," Ashley said.

"I didn't know he was hiring a new dancer," I said, frustrated.

"I know, Music. That's why we're telling you this. You found out about Slyy firing Lisa and hiring a new dancer the same time we did," Ashley replied.

"That explains why everyone's looking at me weird," I said.

"Watch your back," Blanca said, concerned.

"Thanks for letting me know."

"We have been working together for a while, and we consider you family now. Raven is new to this camp and she's being disrespectful," Blanca said, upset.

"I can't believe she would try to break down my credibility. This is beyond disrespectful," I responded, totally irritated, but trying not to let Blanca and Ashley know that I was outraged.

"Why would she start these rumors so quickly?" Ashley asked, confused.

"I don't know," I said.

I knew Raven wanted me out of the picture because no one knew she was a man but me. She must've been afraid her secret would get out.

Raven knew I had found out about the rumors she was spreading, because whenever she saw me, I rolled my eyes at her and didn't care if I was being petty. I wanted her to know I knew what she was up to. I gave her nasty looks and stared at her so long it was making her uncomfortable.

Whenever you saw Slyy, Raven was right by his side. He stopped coming to my room abusing me and gave all his time to Raven. I thought about warning Raven about Slyy, but decided to let her figure it out on her own. I was just relieved he wasn't bothering me anymore.

This business had a strange way of changing people's personality. I would have never thought Raven would treat me the way that she did, especially since we had been friends for so long and experienced so many things together.

Needless to say, touring was too stressful, and it was starting to make me reconsider my hopes and dreams.

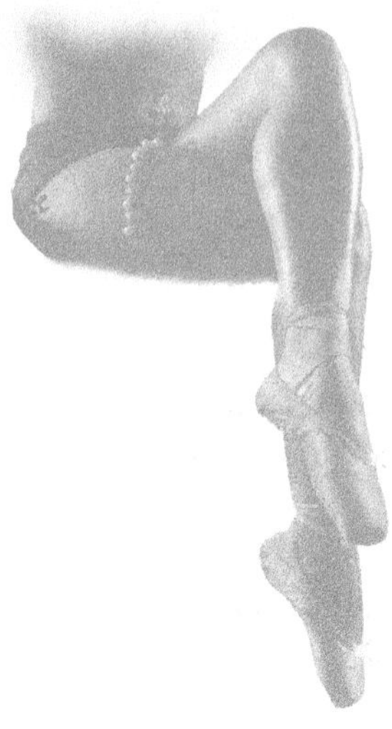

CHAPTER 27

It was the last part of the tour and we were on our way to Japan. We had a long twelve-hour flight, and after five hours of being on the airplane, I was extremely restless and ready to put my feet on solid ground.

Every couple of hours, I had to stretch my legs to keep my blood circulating. I read books, listened to music, watched movies, talked to some of the band members, and slept. I even hung out with Blanca and Ashley to waste time.

I was excited about leaving the country. I even celebrated by having my first taste of Sake, a Japanese rice wine. I enjoyed the experience.

Raven kept trying to talk to me, but I continued ignoring her. I wasn't going to let her ruin my celebration.

"What happened to our friendship?" Raven asked.

"You changed," I responded, while waiting for the restroom to become available.

"I've been a real bitch."

"You can say that again."

"I let my success from modeling go to my head. Do you think you can ever trust me again?" Raven asked sincerely.

"It's hard for me to trust you because I don't know who the hell you are."

"I understand it's going to take time. I'm really sorry, Music."

"I don't know what's up with you," I told her.

"I'm still the same fabulous bitch you love," Raven replied with a smile.

I didn't respond.

"I'm sorry for acting so crazy. You're my best friend and I love you," Raven said.

I still didn't respond.

"Music, do you forgive me?"

"Why should I?"

"Music!" Raven said, as she playfully pushing me.

"Whatever, Raven, but you better not do this shit again," I demanded.

"Thank you. It will never happen again. I'm sorry," Raven responded hugging me tightly.

"I never thought you would treat me this way."

"This business is so enticing. I just got caught up. I saw the gold at the end of the rainbow and went for it."

"You didn't have to stab me in the back to get to the gold."

"I realize now that isn't the way to go."

"You're something else."

"You've always had my back, and I can't trust these bitches in this business. I know you missed me," Raven said, trying to be charming.

"I did miss your crazy butt," I admitted.

"The dynamic duo is back!" Raven said.

I was happy to have my friend back, but I still didn't trust her and would continue to watch my back around her. It was more than her ego that made her treat me that way.

That was a side of Raven I had never seen, and I didn't like it. I knew how to have a working relationship with people, and unfortunately, Raven was added to that list.

In order to enjoy my trip, I would have to pretend to be cool with rekindling our friendship. For some reason, I didn't have a problem doing that. This business was making me become a phony person. Damn, now I was the one changing.

~~~~~~~

We finally made it to Japan and went through customs, showing the officers our passports and worker's permits. The way the officers looked at us made us feel like criminals.

Garrett told us in advance not to say anything smart to the officers because they were serious. I didn't say a word and was through customs in no time.

Slyy's stylist made a smart comment to the officer, asking him, "Why are you looking at me like that?" Of course, they told him to step to the side. Garrett kept looking at him, trying to get him to be quiet, but he kept talking. So, they escorted him to a back room.

"Are you going to go see if he's alright?" We asked Garrett.

"Hell no!" He replied. "I told him not to say anything. Now his mouth got his ass in trouble. He's on his own."

We picked up our luggage and kept moving. I continued looking back to see if the stylist was going to emerge from the room, but he never did. They finally released him hours later.

Japan was beautiful, and the hotel was so clean you could eat off the floor. It was a five-star hotel, and you could feel it as soon as you stepped in the lobby. The hotel staff was kind and professional, and we were checked in with no wait. We were given a complimentary silk Kimono and a huge welcome basket.

The rooms were beautiful with a unique Japanese décor. The bathroom was also very distinctive. With a push of a button, the shower curtains opened and the shower turned on. You could even adjust the temperature by
~~~~~~~

remote control. You could also make a telephone call in surround sound.

I called Blanca and asked, "How do you like your room?"

"I love it," she replied.

"I'm sitting on the heated toilet," I told her, while laughing.

Blanca laughed with me and said, "Me too!"

Together, we called Ashley, Raven, and a couple of the band members, connecting everyone on the phone at once. We were all sitting on the toilet playing with the gadgets.

So far, I loved Japan. However, when I picked up the telephone to place an order with room service, I couldn't understand the operator because she was speaking Japanese. I knew Japan was too good to be true.

Frustrated and hungry, I went to the hotel lobby and spoke with the hotel concierge who spoke English.

"I'm trying to order food from room service, but they don't speak English. Can you help me?" I asked desperately.

"Sure. I can read the menu to you and place your order."

After hearing the food options on the menu, I decided I wanted something simple and familiar to eat.

"Are there any places around the hotel to get a hamburger?" I asked the concierge.

"There's a restaurant a few blocks from here that sells hamburgers."

"Thank you!" I said excited.

I immediately got the directions from her and made some calls to see if anyone was hungry.

"I know where we can get some hamburgers. Do you want to go?" I asked Blanca as soon as she picked up the telephone.

"Yes. I'm starving," she said.

"Call Ashley and Raven, then meet me in the lobby."

"Okay, I'll see you in five minutes," Blanca said.

While I was waiting, I converted fifty U.S. dollars to Japanese yen. While the concierge was giving me a quick lesson on converting money, Raven, Ashley, Blanca, and a few band members gathered in the lobby. They were hungry and happy there was a restaurant that sold hamburgers close by.

We found the restaurant with no problem and immediately ordered hamburgers and fries. Once the food arrived, no one said a word until we finished. Some of the band members even ordered extra hamburgers to take back to the hotel with them.

Full and happy, we headed back to the hotel to get some much-needed rest. We had jetlag from the long plane ride, and now that we had eaten, sleep was kicking in.

~~~~~~~

We were at sound check for our first show Japan. The club provided food, drinks, and even a huge welcome cake for our arrival.

"Thanks for the food. It was great," I told our escort, Kameko.

"You're welcome. You guys can really eat," she said, laughing.

"We're hungry," I replied.

"We don't eat as much as Americans do," Kameko told me.

"Why do you think we eat so much?" I asked.

"We eat small portions of food, and you guys eat large portions. Americans are overweight."

"What do you mean?"

"Americans can eat two to three slices of bacon. For us, one slice of bacon is two slices," she said.

"Now that you explained it like that, we are pigs!" I said, laughing.

Our first show was at a club in Osaka, Japan, and we were booked to perform there every night for one week.

"Five minutes to show time," Garrett announced.
~~~~~~~

"Are we having a show tonight?" I asked Garrett.

"Yes. Didn't you hear me say five minutes to show time?" he snapped.

"One day, I'm going to knock the hell out of him," I mumbled to myself.

I didn't hear a sound from the audience and was beginning to think no one came to the show. We headed to the side of the stage, said our prayer, and waited to go on.

Raven and I peeked out of the curtains to see the audience. The club was filled to capacity and the show was sold out. The weirdest thing was the audience was completely silent.

"Why are they so quiet?" Raven asked Kameko.

"This is our custom. It's disrespectful to make noise before a show starts," she replied.

"Are they going to continue to stay quiet during the entire show?" I inquired.

"No. Once the show starts, they will make noise and enjoy it, but until then, they will remain silent."

"Wow!" Raven and I said in unison.

After the show started, the audience began clapping and singing along with the songs. I felt like I was at a party and not performing.

At the end of the show, we invited some of the audience on the stage to dance with us. The show turned out to be fun and unusual. When it was over, the crowd asked for autographs and made us feel like rock stars.

They wanted to take pictures and were happy to get a chance to just touch us. There were so many people that we had to be escorted to our dressing room. Japan is great!

The night of our third show, we were introduced to Lady Mam, who was an extremely wealthy and well-known businesswoman in Japan. She owned several restaurants and hotels in Hiroshima, Tokyo, and Osaka. She was accompanied by three beautiful women named Akira, Takara, and Yuriko, who immediately told us they were professional dancers.

Lady Mam invited our entire entourage to one of her restaurants and had three limousines waiting for us outside of the club. After accepting her invitation, the whole crew was taken to a very posh restaurant.

The restaurant was beautiful and the food was incredible. Lady Mam made sure Slyy was pampered and catered to the entire night. She also invited all the dancers to visit her hotel spa to get massages. We eagerly agreed.

Two weeks later, and the morning before our last show in Osaka, Slyy made a big announcement to us.

"I've hired three new dancers."

"Who?" Everyone asked.

"I've hired the three girls that Lady Mam introduced us to. I think they will add a new flare to the show," Slyy said proudly.

By now, we were used to Slyy switching things up and weren't shocked by his announcement. We didn't know why he hired more dancers with only a few shows left on the tour, but we went along with it and welcomed them to the group.

Our final show of the tour that would be in Los Angeles was going to be televised. The program was going to be a special all about Slyy's life on the road. We knew the televised show was the reason he hired new dancers at the end of his tour.

"I want to do something exclusive for the television show," Slyy said.

"How are they going to learn the routines in such a short time?" Ashley asked.

"They have been at every show studying the routines, and they will perform with us tonight," Slyy replied.

"Why do we need new dancers?" Blanca asked.

"Because I like them and think they will be a good addition to my show."

I knew it had nothing to do with their dancing skills. He saw three beautiful, sexy women that he was attracted to and wanted them around him.

"I'm sending you guys to buy new outfits for the show tonight. I want you all to look good," Slyy said, handing Raven his credit card.

"Wow, new outfits!" Raven said, smiling from ear to ear.

"Lady Mam's limousine is waiting to take you guys to her boutique. Buy something sexy for the show. The new dancers will meet you there," Slyy informed us.

"We're getting new dancers and new outfits," Blanca responded sarcastically.

"Just be happy you're getting new outfits," Slyy said.

"I'm happy," Raven stated.

"The limousine is waiting for you guys. Hurry up and get back on time," Slyy said.

We met the new dancers at the boutique, and they were very friendly. They were beautiful with an exotic look and made us look like ugly ducklings. One of the dancers named Akira spoke English fairly well and was the leader of the pack. She spoke on behalf of Takara and Yuriko.

Blanca and Ashley immediately started asking them about their dance experience while we looked through the boutique for outfits.

"How long have you guys been dancing?" Ashley asked.

"We've been dancing for many years," Akira said.

"Are you trained dancers?" Blanca asked.

"Takara is a trained dancer, but Yuriko and I are self-taught," Akira replied.

I was thrilled to hear her say they were self-taught dancers. I definitely could relate to them. I knew Blanca and Ashley were not going to respect them, but I had much respect for any self-taught dancer.

"What entertainers have you worked for?" Blanca asked.

"We have never danced with entertainers from the United States, but we have danced with many entertainers from Japan," Akira told us.

Blanca and Ashley still were not impressed, and it showed on their faces.

"It really doesn't matter what dance experience they have because they're dancing tonight at the show," I said, annoyed with Blanca and Ashley's attitude.

Raven didn't believe they had the routines already and asked, "Don't you guys need to rehearse?"

"No. We just need to know our position on stage," Akira answered calmly.

Raven couldn't wait until sound check to see if they could keep up with us.

"I hope Slyy isn't trying to replace us. Seven dancers on stage, is just too many people," Raven said, as I pulled her to the side.

"We need to step up our game to keep our job secure," I told her.

We purchased seven hot outfits and then headed back to sound check. Once there, we figured out our position on stage to incorporate seven dancers. As the band played the first song, we stared at the new dancers to see why they were hired.

They nailed every song perfectly and did the choreography better than we did. We looked at each other amazed, but were not going to let them outshine us.

"You guys are really good," I told them.

"Thanks. We worked really hard," Akira said.

"Make sure you bitches know who the head dancers are," Raven said jokingly.

"We were told there are no head dancers," Akira responded with a sneaky smile.

Raven didn't know what to say in response to her comment, so she remained silent. Ashley and I looked at each other and raised our eyebrows. I knew Akira had a little fire in her and knew she would fit in perfectly with us.

Three hours later, Garrett yelled, "It's show time!"

The new dancers made us dance harder on stage, while they did the choreography easily. We were amazed at their skills and had to give them respect because they were fantastic.

"How did you learn the routines so perfectly?" Raven asked them after the show.

"We videotaped the first show and have been rehearsing every day to perfect it," Akira said.

"Why did you start rehearsing the show before you were hired?" Ashley inquired.

"That's how we get jobs. We learn the choreography, Lady Mam sets up the meeting, and the rest is history," Akira said.

"You guys planned this?" I asked.

"Absolutely," she responded.

"How did you know Slyy would hire you?" Raven asked curiously.

"Men can't resist us. They see a sexy, beautiful woman first before they see a professional dancer. And who wouldn't want us?" Akira replied with confidence.

"Damn! Now that's a hustle I'm going to use," Raven said, giving Akira respect.

"I didn't think they had hustlers in Japan," I stated.

"Well, now you know," Akira said, smiling.

A few minutes later, Slyy came into our dressing room. "You guys did a great job and looked good together. I couldn't believe how well you did the choreography. I'm happy you're working with me. Make sure you have your passports because you'll be coming with me," Slyy said, smiling.

Akira, Yuriko, and Takara walked over to Slyy and gave him a seductive kiss on his cheek.

"Thanks, Slyy," they said.

"Just don't let me down," he told them.

"We'll make sure you're very pleased. You won't regret hiring us," Akira responded.

"When we get to Los Angeles, I'm going to create a whole new performance, and we will prepare for the last big show of the tour. After the last show, we will have six months off while I finish my new album. Then we will start rehearsal for my new tour," Slyy informed us. "Que will be producing some songs for me, and I'm going to add him to my next tour to promote his album."

I was happy to hear that their meeting worked out for Que, but I still hated Slyy and was trying to figure out a way to talk to Que about it.

Slyy then turned to me and said, "Thanks for hooking me up with Que."

"You're welcome," I replied.

"During the six months off, I'll have a few spot dates every month," he said to us.

"I'm happy we'll still be making money until the new tour starts," Raven commented.

"I want everyone to stay and continue to work with me. That's why I will be keeping you busy during your break."

I was happy to hear we would be getting time off and still making money. I really needed a break from the road and time to think about if I wanted to continue working with Slyy.

"We will be wearing new outfits for the last show. The men will wear white tuxedoes, and the ladies will wear long, white, flowing dresses. The stage will be white, and I'm renting all-white equipment," Slyy told us.

"That sounds great," Blanca said, interrupting him.

"I want my last show to leave a lasting impression on everyone. Everyone will be interviewed, so get ready," he said with excitement.

While we were in Japan, the televised show was being promoted on every radio station and was already sold out. We finished the rest of the overseas tour traveling to Germany, Switzerland, Paris, and Europe.

A few weeks later, we were on our way back to Los Angeles, and the new dancers were with us. They stayed to themselves and didn't say much.

When we arrived in Los Angeles, we had two days off before the last show, but one of those days we had to rehearse.

"If you guys need any help, let me know. I know you are in a new place," I said to Akira, as we checked into the hotel.

"Thanks, Music. I appreciate it," she replied.

"Maybe we can go and hang out," I said.

"That would be cool."

Touring is rough and you never really have a life. I hadn't been on a date in a long time, and I really just wanted to do something normal, like go to the movies. Living my life on the road, I never had time to do anything and my life revolved around Slyy.

Usually, you could act silly on stage and play practical jokes on the last show of a tour. However, Slyy didn't believe in this foolishness, especially since his last show was going to be televised. Therefore, there would be no playing around on stage.

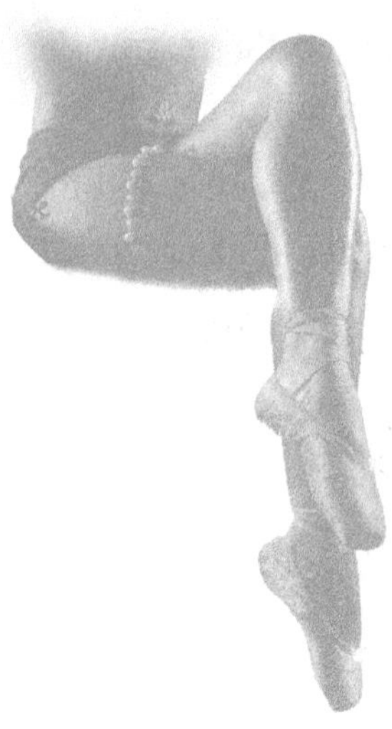

CHAPTER 28

Janice was filming a movie and wasn't able to travel to Japan with us, but she came to the rehearsal for the televised show to meet Raven and the new dancers.

As Blanca filled Janice in on things that happened on the road, Janice was like a pit bull ready to attack Raven. She never said anything to Slyy about being unfaithful, but would harass the women she thought was sleeping with him, which was any woman on the tour.

This time she had met her match, because Raven didn't care that Janice was Slyy's fiancée. She was still going to keep hanging around him and getting anything she wanted.

I thought Raven was going to act differently when Janice came around, but she didn't. She was milking Slyy for his money, and he was giving it to her easily.

Normally, I would have some negative things to say about what Raven was doing, but because it was Slyy she was using, I didn't care. I didn't know how much money Raven was getting from him until we arrived in Los Angeles.

Raven was living large, shopping on Rodeo Drive, all at Slyy's expense. She had him right where she wanted him, wrapped around her finger. Slyy had done so many people wrong, especially me, therefore, I was happy someone was doing him wrong.

Slyy even bought Raven a condo in Los Angeles before she started touring with us. He bought her a newly-built, two-level, three-bedroom condo and a new Mercedes Benz. Raven and Slyy had been together before she started dancing on his tour.

Raven invited Blanca, Ashley, and me to her condo in Beverly Hills, and as soon as she opened the door, we were impressed. Raven was living lavish. Her condo was expensively decorated, and she had the best of everything.

Looking at her condo, luxury car, and expensive clothing, it was obvious she was well taken care of. In private, she showed her bank statements to me, and it reflected a large amount in her savings account, proving she was definitely financially set.

"You have a really nice place," Blanca said, surprised.

"When did you get this condo?" Ashley asked.

"I bought it a few months before I started the tour," Raven answered.

"Somebody is treating you good," Ashley said, as Raven looked at her but didn't comment.

"How did you get all of this on a dancer's salary?" Blanca asked.

"A woman never tells her secrets," Raven replied, smiling.

"Show us the rest of your condo," I said, trying to stop them from asking so many questions.

She showed off her entire condo to us, and it was absolutely beautiful. Blanca and Ashley continued to question Raven about her personal life, while Raven kept ignoring them.

"Can I have something to drink?" Ashley asked.

"Sure. I have bottled water in the refrigerator and some potato chips in the cabinet," Raven said.

"Great! We're going to raid your refrigerator," Blanca replied, as they walked into the kitchen.

Raven and I headed to her bedroom so she could pack her clothes. Even though she had a condo in Los Angeles, Slyy wanted everyone to check into a hotel the day of the show.

He wanted to finish the tour like we started it, staying in hotels and meeting in the lobby before the show.

This way he knew everyone would be on time. We had to be checked into the hotel by ten o'clock that night and could not check out until after the show.

"This is really a nice place," I said.

"It's fabulous!" Raven bragged.

"You're working his pockets," I commented with a smile.

"What are you talking about?"

"You know what I'm talking about. You're taking Slyy's money."

Raven laughed. "Girl, it was so easy. He's a typical man."

"Have you guys slept together?"

"No, but we have fooled around a couple of times. I've given him some serious head, and now he's hooked."

"You know he's going to want to have sex with you."

"He thinks we're going to have sex, but he'll be fooled when I pull out this one-eyed snake and ram it up his ass."

"Girl, you're crazy. You better be careful dating these straight men and trying to turn them out."

"I know what I'm doing. He's not my type, but I love his money."

"Did you know he's engaged to Janice?" I asked.

"I don't care about Janice. She should know the type of man that she's marrying. She can have him once I finish getting what I need from him," Raven replied, as she put on a diamond ring and bracelet.

"He's a horrible person," I said, while contemplating if I should tell her what Slyy had been done to me.

"I know he's a dirty man, and that's why I'm taking his money," Raven responded.

Blanca and Ashley walked in the bedroom, just when I was about to tell her about Slyy.

"Are you guys ready to go?" Ashley asked, as she stuffed some potato chips in her mouth.

"I'm ready to go shopping. We only have today to shop and get ready for the show since we have to rehearse all day tomorrow," Blanca reminded us.

"Let's go," Raven said, grabbing the keys to the car.

We headed out the door to shop on Rodeo Drive.

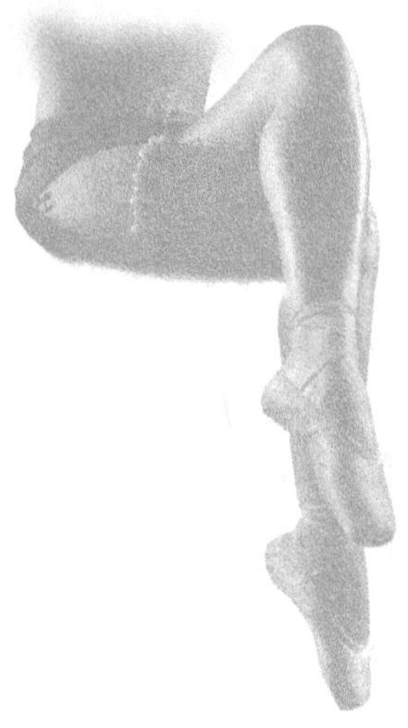

CHAPTER 29

Que and I were the first to arrive in the lobby of the hotel, ready to finish the last show of the tour. Que was scheduled to sing in a special section of the show created just for him, and he couldn't wait to perform.

This was going to be a huge stepping stone for Que's career, and he was hyped about their collaboration.

"What's up, baby?" Que said, giving me a kiss on the cheek.

"You look good," I told him.

"Thanks. So do you."

"We would look good as a couple," he stated.

"Now you know that's not going to happen."

"You never know what can happen."

"I love the all-white theme," I said, trying to change the subject.

"This show is going to be hot! Wait until you see the white outfit I'm going to perform in," Que replied, then popped a pill in his mouth.

"Are you still popping pills? I told you to go to the dentist."

"I'm going once the tour is over. But, for now, I need this Vicodin because my tooth is killing me."

"We have to wear all white to arrive at the show and then change into another all-white outfit to perform in. That's too much," I said.

"Slyy knows what he's doing. We definitely will make an impression when everyone walks in with all white. Don't forget the rehearsal for my tour will be starting soon. So make sure you're ready," Que reminded me.

"I'm ready to go," I replied.

"I'm very strict when it comes to rehearsal. I'm a different person, and I hope you can handle that," Que said seriously.

"I can handle anything now."

"I hope so, because I like things my way," he forewarned me.

"You were like that as a kid. You always wanted your way."

"I'm a grown man now, and doing it my way can feel good to you."

"What are you talking about?" I asked, confused.

"Don't act naïve."

"You're always talking about sex," I said.

"Is Raven going to dance for my tour," he asked.

"I've already hooked that up for you."

"I have four dancers already who have been working with me from the beginning of my solo career, so you guys will be joining them."

"Six dancers! You're creating a big show," I said, amazed.

"Bigger than I have ever done before, so don't fuck up my show," he responded with a serious tone.

"You know I'm going to work it," I said with confidence.

We continued to talk while waiting for everyone to arrive in the hotel lobby.

"Can't you find another color other than white to wear?" Ashley asked laughing.

"We look so good. Let's take a picture," Blanca said.

"I can't wait to see us in our white outfits for the show. This was a good idea," Ashley said.

"Where's Raven?" I asked Blanca.

"She's probably on her way down now," she replied.

We were all in great spirits, and it felt like the last time we would see each other. The last day of the tour was always difficult. It's hard to say goodbye.

All you heard was laughing and talking coming from the hotel lobby while we waited for the rest of the crew. When the hotel's elevator doors opened, Raven stepped out looking amazing.

She had on a white fitted dress that had diamond cluster straps. On her feet were white, strappy, diamond stilettos, and she was drenched in diamonds. She walked out of the elevators looking confident, powerful, and rich.

"You look great," Que said, complimenting Raven.

"Thanks," Raven replied.

"I want you to dance for me on my tour," Que told her.

"I wouldn't miss it for the world," Raven told him.

"You really look beautiful," Que said, while licking his lips.

"Thanks. You look very handsome," Raven said, flirting back.

"I've got to have you," Que added.

"Maybe you will, maybe you won't," Raven answered, then walked away smiling.

We surrounded Raven and complimented her on her outfit. Five minutes later, Slyy and Janice walked out of the elevator. We did a double take when we saw Janice had on the exact same outfit, shoes, and diamonds that Raven was wearing. We started laughing under our breath.

We knew Slyy had bought the outfits for Raven and Janice, but we couldn't believe he would buy them the exact same ensemble for this special occasion. Slyy was getting too comfortable with his fiancé and mistress.

Ashley and I were laughing so hard that we had to walk away to compose ourselves. It only took Janice a few seconds to spot Raven and realize they looked like identical twins from head to toe.

She looked upset, yet embarrassed because she knew everyone saw what was going on. On the other hand, Raven wasn't concerned. She looked at Janice and then looked away laughing inside. She had no remorse.

"This is a damn shame," I whispered in Raven's ear.

"I don't care. He's stupid to buy us the same outfit," Raven replied.

"Slyy is wrong," I told her.

"That's why I'm using his no-good ass," Raven said.

"Maybe you should change your outfit," I suggested.

"I'm not changing. Slyy created this mess. My whole look today cost over five thousand dollars, and I'm going to wear this outfit tonight," Raven responded with an attitude.

Everyone got in the stretch white limousines on our way to the show. It was weird hearing them gossip about Raven, because for once on this tour, they were not talking about me.

Raven started feeling tense because this was not the type of spotlight she wanted to be in. For a second, I felt sad for her, but she knew what she was doing. She didn't care how it looked, so why should I?

When we arrived at the show, everyone was still talking about Janice and Raven's outfits. Slyy had taught Raven what to do and how to act while Janice was around, so this didn't faze her. Janice appeared humiliated and looked like she wanted to kill Raven.

Janice was wasting her time trying to scare Raven off, because she wasn't going anywhere until she got everything she wanted from Slyy. She knew how men ticked. Hell, she *was* a man. Raven and Slyy's relationship wasn't a secret anymore; it was out in the open.

The backstage area was crowded, and there were television stations filming while waiting for Slyy's arrival. Every entertainer you could think of was at the show. Even the backstage area was decorated with white, flowing curtains and white roses.

Before we could get in the door, a film crew was in our face asking us questions about working Slyy. Garrett had prepared us for the interviews by telling us what to say and what not to say. We were on point and ready to answer any questions. We shook people's hands, took tons of pictures, and were interviewed before we got to our dressing room.

It was a madhouse backstage, and we were relieved to be in our dressing room. Slyy didn't get a break and had a film crew in his dressing room capturing his every move.

Once the door to our dressing room closed, it was quickly opened again by another film crew ready to interview us.

"What is it like dancing for Slyy?" A reporter asked me.

"It's exciting and rewarding," I answered, while gritting my teeth because these were not my words.

"How many years have you been working with Slyy?" They asked Raven.

"I've only been with him for a few months, but I feel like family," she said.

They continued asking question after question, and it felt like it would never end. Garrett prepared us for every question they could possibly ask, so we knew exactly what to say.

"Tell us a scary situation on the road," the reporter asked Blanca.

"We had a stalker, but Slyy took care of everything," she responded.

"Tell us something no one knows about Slyy," was the reporter's next request.

"He's a really nice guy and good to his staff," Ashley replied.

Even though they asked each of us different questions, we had the perfect answers to give them. Every answer was perfectly written. We knew better than to screw it up, because this was a big day for Slyy.

The reporters interviewed Garrett, the tour bus drivers, stylists, and crew members. They even filmed the tour bus inside and out. They wanted footage of everything that had something to do with Slyy's life.

All the questions were starting to make me tired, and I hadn't even performed yet. I couldn't see how celebrities did this all the time.

It was almost show time, and Slyy had everyone that was a part of the tour come to his dressing room to give us a pep talk.

"This is an important show, and a lot of key people are in the audience. I'm happy to work with each of you because you're like family to me."

We paid attention to what he was saying.

"I know I've been rough on you guys. I'm sorry for anything I might have done to hurt you, but I'm not a perfect man," Slyy said, as he looked directly at me.

I put my head down, and Janice looked at him like she didn't believe a word he was saying.

"I trust you guys, and I want you to continue to work with me. The future looks great, and I want you guys to be a part of it," he added.

After having seen the good and bad side of Slyy, none of us had told any of his secrets, and for that, he was grateful. Slyy got choked up while talking to us, but I didn't know if he was being truthful or just playing it up for the cameras that were filming his speech.

Everyone was quiet while he spoke because he seemed very humble and his speech seemed so sincere. When he was speaking, he looked directly into people's eyes, somehow trying to clear his conscious.

Once Slyy was done, Garrett handed each of us a glass of champagne and said, "Let's toast to a new beginning and a start of something bigger and better."

We toasted and drank together.

"For the last time on this tour, it's thirty minutes to show time!" Garrett yelled.

We hugged each other and were now pumped up for the show.

Before we left, Slyy said, "Have a great show, and let's show them what we're made of."

We clapped as we left his dressing room. This was a special moment in time, and it was all captured on film.

The crowd was roaring, people were taking pictures, and the cameras were still filming our every step. We waited on the side of the stage for the last time. I felt sad, but knew we would be doing it all over again in six months.

As Slyy said a prayer, everyone's eyes filled with tears. He ended his prayer by saying, "Thank you guys for making this a wonderful and successful tour."

Slyy's white suit had diamonds on the collar, and he even had a white diamond microphone and stand, made especially for the show.

While the band played the first song, we followed Slyy on the stage. The crowd went ballistic when they saw the full stage decorated in all white and the entire crew in white. Before Slyy started singing, he stopped the band to talk to the audience.

"Welcome and thank you for coming. I really appreciate all of you."

The crowd's response was overwhelming. They wouldn't settle down, so Slyy continued the show.

This show seemed livelier than any other show we had done, and the crowd and cameras were enjoying every minute of it.

Towards the middle of the show, I looked on the side of the stage and saw Garrett flinging his hands in the air trying to get Slyy's attention. When he looked towards Garrett, he held a sign up that said, "Bomb threat!"

Everyone on stage saw the sign, but we continued dancing and the band continued playing. We were used to the bomb threats; it didn't faze us anymore. However, Slyy stopped singing in the middle of the song and signaled for the band to stop playing.

He didn't want anything to jeopardize his show because he had worked so hard planning it. So, he knew he had to handle the situation correctly since it was all being filmed.

Although we had been through this before and it was always a false alarm, it still frightened us. Slyy took a long, deep breath and started talking to the audience.

"I don't want to alarm you, but there is another bomb threat."

Of course, the audience started to panic.

"Relax and calm down!" Slyy said.

He explained to the audience in detail about Bubba making the bomb threats. Slyy said very loudly, "I'm not afraid of Bubba, and I'm tired of him interrupting my shows!"

The crowd ended up staying and listened to Slyy as he continued talking. When he was done, he said, "If you want to leave, than leave, but the show will go on. Bubba will not win tonight!"

The audience started shouting different comments.

"We love you, Slyy!"

"We're not scared!"

"Go on with the show!"

"Start the show!" The audience repeatedly chanted.

A huge smile came across Slyy's face, then he gave the band the cue and they started playing right on his command.

The audience continued enjoying the show like nothing ever happened. The cameras loved the bomb threat speech. It would definitely be front-page news.

The show was a hit, and the audience loved Que's addition. On the last song of the show, a small explosion went off and confetti fell onto the stage.

When the show was over, the audience started yelling, "Encore!"

Slyy granted their wish by performing another song, and he invited Que on stage to join him. As they sang a ballad off Slyy's album, the crowd was mesmerized.

Slyy told the audience they would hear a lot more from Que. With the audience wanting more, they did a song off Que's album.

Then for the last time on this tour, we took a bow and said, "Goodnight."

It was extremely crowded trying to exit the stage, and the film crew was in the way with their cameras. Garrett instructed everyone to stay in their dressing rooms because we were not done filming and had a few more interviews to do.

"I need some time alone in my dressing room, so make sure no one bothers me for a while," Slyy told Garrett.

"I'll take care of it," Garrett replied.

"Don't let people know I'm in my dressing room. Tell them I'm doing an interview in another room," Slyy said.

We went back to our room, changed clothes, reapplied our makeup, freshened up, and kicked off our shoes to relax. After waiting in the dressing room, we were ready to mingle.

It was like one big happy party backstage. People were talking, eating, drinking, and socializing, so we joined the crowd.

With all the A-list people, it was media heaven backstage. There were some media that didn't have access, so they had to wait outside the backstage door, where it was just as crazy as inside. People were everywhere, and the cameras continued to film.

So many pictures were taken of me that my cheeks were tired from smiling and my feet were killing me from dancing in four-inch heels all night.

The cameras and reporters surrounded Janice, not giving her a break. They wanted to know everything about her life. They were so persistent that Slyy's security had to escort her around.

With the word buzzing around that Slyy had won a Grammy, the media couldn't take enough pictures or do enough interviews regarding it. We were celebrating having a great tour and more great tours to come.

CHAPTER 30

Ending the tour with a great show made everyone pleased. Raven, Que and I continued to hang out backstage enjoying the moment.

"Music, I'm sorry for treating you wrong. Can you forgive me?" Raven asked.

"I've already forgiven you in Japan," I responded.

"I know. I just felt like asking again. I love you, girl," Raven said.

"I love you, too," I replied.

"Stop all the mushy talk," Que said, smiling. "I just want you both to be ready to do my tour."

"I'm always ready," Raven responded, smiling back at Que.

"I bet you are," Que said, flirting with her.

"Let's toast to my tour being just as successful as Slyy's tour," Que said, raising his glass of Champagne in the air.

As we toasted and hugged each other, Blanca and Ashley joined in our conversation.

"We've been through so much on this tour, and I'm happy that we became friends," Blanca expressed.

"Let's toast to more money, more money, and more money!" Ashley said.

We hugged, put our glasses in the air, and toasted again to our friendship, more shows, and more money. I also toasted to Akira, Takara, and Yuriko, because when they joined the tour, they made us become closer as friends.

It was the best night of my life and I felt great. It was a good way to end the tour. After Blanca and Ashley walked away to do more interviews, we continued talking and laughing.

"What's it like touring with Slyy?" Que asked.

"It's okay," Raven and I said, as we looked at each other and twisted our lips.

"What do you mean by that?" Que asked.

"We'll tell you the details later," I said.

At that very moment, I decided I would confide in Que and tell him what type of person Slyy really was.

"Do you guys like touring?"

"Yes. Touring gives you the opportunity to travel the world and experience things you never would have gotten a chance to," Raven answered.

"You do get a chance to see the world," Que added.

"I have seen in person the Royal Palace and the Eiffel Tower. I've even met the President, hung out with movie stars and shopped at the most exclusive boutiques in the world. I've definitely had some wonderful times, but also some bad ones while on tour," I said, reminiscing.

"Touring has been everything I've expected and more," Raven said.

"Come with me to Slyy's dressing room. I want to hang out with him for a moment," Que said.

Raven and I didn't want to go, but Que insisted.

"Come on. I won't be long," Que told us.

"Okay, but we're not staying long," I told him.

Laughing and talking, we went with Que to Slyy's dressing room. No one even noticed as we and walked right in since his security was still busy escorting Janice around backstage.

Slyy was in his dressing room alone, sitting on the couch eating steak, potatoes, and drinking a glass of Champagne. Since no one knew he was in his room, he was able to relax. He was drunk and didn't seem to care that we walked in without knocking or being escorted by his security.

"Hello, guys," Slyy said, appearing excited to see us.

"Sorry for interrupting you, but I just wanted to say hello," Que said.

"No problem. Come on in."

"Thanks," we said.

"Do you guys want something to eat?" Slyy asked.

"Yes," we replied, sounding like a chorus.

We dug in like we hadn't eaten in days, eating steak and potatoes with him, while Slyy started talking about how great the show was and how he couldn't wait to get started on his next tour.

"The show was great!" Que said.

"I was very pleased. Everyone looked good and sounded great," Slyy commented, while drinking champagne.

"The dancers were also great," Que said.

"My dancers are loyal to me and I respect them."

That's when Que told him, "I want to take Music and Raven on tour with me."

Slyy looked a little stunned and boldly said, "I don't share dancers."

"Don't be stingy. We're family," Que responded while flashing a huge smile.

"These girls are my family," Slyy said, as he continued to eat and drink. He hesitated for a moment before saying, "You're my boy, so I guess you can borrow them for your tour."

"Borrow?" Que replied, laughing.

"Make sure you return my girls when I need them."

Frowning, Raven and I listened to them talk about us like we were a pair of shoes.

Slyy looked over at us and asked, "What's wrong with you guys?"

We both shook our heads annoyed.

"You act like you own us," Raven said.

"I do own you," Slyy responded with authority.

"You don't own me!" Raven snapped.

I knew he was drunk, so I didn't want to get into this conversation with him. Seeing that we were getting uncomfortable, Que tried to stop Slyy from continuing.

"We sounded great tonight," Que told Slyy, trying to change the subject.

"I own all my dancers!" Slyy said, still wanting to continue the conversation.

"Slyy, you don't own anybody," Raven shot back.

Que started laughing, as he continued eating his steak. Slyy became furious. He didn't like Raven making him look like he wasn't in control, especially in front of Que.

When Que realized Slyy was upset, he tried to calm him down. "They know you're running things."

Slyy wasn't trying to hear it. The liquor had set in, and he was ready to explode. As soon as the crazy look appeared in his eyes, I knew it was time to go.

I put my plate on the table and told Raven, "It's time to go," as I grabbed her arm and pulled her towards the door.

"Where are you going?" Slyy asked.

"We're getting out of here," I answered.

"Sit down now!" Slyy ordered, while jumping up.

"Slyy, you need to relax," Raven told him.

"Don't tell me what to do," Slyy said angrily.

"You're drunk! Now chill out!" Raven yelled.

"Who the hell are you talking to?" Slyy asked.

Next thing anyone knew, Slyy had pushed Raven, and she tripped and fell on the floor.

"What are you doing?" Que asked, stunned as he jumped up to help Raven.

"Stay out of this," Slyy snapped.

"Stop, Slyy! You're drunk," I said.

Slyy quickly turned around and slapped me so hard that I fell and knocked all the food and silverware off the table and onto the floor.

"Don't tell me what to do!" Slyy shouted.

As Raven rushed over to help me, Que immediately jumped up in Slyy's face enrage. "What the fuck are you doing? I think you need to calm down!"

Slyy just looked at him.

"Only punks hit women," Que said gritting his teeth.

"You need to stay in your place," Slyy said very slowly.

"I will beat your ass. You don't touch Music!" Que warned him, ready to swing.

"It's not worth it, Que. Let's just go," Raven yelled, while trying to help me up from the floor. When Raven saw that Que wasn't moving, she grabbed his arm and tried to separate them. "Que, let's go!"

I started thinking about all the times Slyy had hit and raped me. Now he was hitting me in front of my friends. I was embarrassed and couldn't stop crying.

"Get the fuck out of my room!" Slyy shouted.

"You're a punk! Let's go, Music!" Que said.

"This ain't your business," Slyy replied.

Que was fuming as Slyy walked over to me and grabbed my arm.

"You leave when I tell you to," Slyy told me.

Before I could respond, Que grabbed Slyy's arm and twisted it. "I told you not to touch her."

Slyy snatched his arm away from him. "Boy, I told you to mind your business."

"I'm not a boy. Don't test me," Que warned.

"You're big and bad now?" Slyy asked, laughing.

"And you're a punk-ass bitch."

Before Que could finish his sentence, Slyy swung and hit him in his jaw. Que instantly swung back hard, hitting Slyy in his chest and knocking him to the floor. Then Slyy grabbed Que's legs and pulled him on the floor with him.

Raven and I didn't know why this was happening when it was supposed to be a friendly visit. We had only been in the room for ten minutes and things had gotten out of control that quick.

After Slyy managed to stand up, he began kicking Que in his ribs. I tried to stop him from hurting Que, but he pushed me away, while Raven kept screaming for him to stop.

With all the talking and music blasting, no one in the backstage area heard what was going on in Slyy's dressing room.

While Slyy was telling Raven to shut up and pushing me off of him, Que grabbed a steak knife off the floor and lunged at Slyy. He held the knife firmly in his hand and stuck it deep into his neck. Slyy fell to the floor in pain.

"Que, what did you do?" Raven asked, panicking.

Que didn't respond. He just stood still trying to catch his breath.

It felt like the room was spinning and I was in the middle of a tornado.

"I'm tired of the rapes and beatings," I blurted out, while continuing to cry.

"What?" Raven and Que said in unison, surprised by my words.

I'm not sure why I decided at that moment to share my secret, but it just flowed out of me.

"What are you talking about?" Raven asked, as she cried with me.

Que was in shock as he kept looking at Slyy and then back at me.

"This motherfucker raped and beat you?" Que shouted.

I was so irate I couldn't speak.

"Music, why didn't you tell me this before I started working with this piece of shit?" Que yelled.

"I didn't want to mess up your opportunity to work with him. I know that was your dream," I answered through tears.

"Fuck a dream! This motherfucker was doing that to you all this time and you didn't tell me? Music, what were you thinking? What the fuck is going on?" Que asked furiously.

Slyy was lying on the floor holding his neck, while blood rapidly oozed.

"You bastard!" Raven said and then kicked Slyy in his ribs, causing him to holler out in pain. "You're a fucking pig!" She added.

"I hate you!" I said, than joined Raven in kicking him again.

Kicking him felt so good and allowed me to release all my anger. Slyy couldn't speak and was struggling to breathe, choking on his own blood.

"Stop, Music! I think he's really hurt," Raven said, as she stopped me.

When we saw that Slyy wasn't moving and how much blood he had lost, we realized how seriously he was injured. That's when I started to panic. We looked at each other for answers on what to do next.

Raven immediately snapped out of her trance. "We need to get the hell out of here."

Que looked at me and I looked at Raven fearfully.

Suddenly, Que's survival mode kicked in. He grabbed a towel off the floor, walked over to Slyy, wrapped the towel around the handle of the knife, and quickly pulled it out of his neck.

Slyy wailed and his eyes started popping out of his head, while he continued to struggle to breathe. His body was jerking as the blood continued to squirt out of his neck.

Raven and I stood in silence watching Que. He started wiping the handle of the knife off, and when he was done, he dropped the knife next to Slyy.

In a serious tone, he turned to us and said, "Let's get the hell out of here. Don't mention a word to anyone. Let's walk out of this room the same way we came in, laughing and talking," Que said.

We didn't ask any questions. We just listened to our instructions.

"When you leave this room, get a plate of food. I will mingle with the crowd. We will meet back up a little later. Stay close."

I was so scared that I was shaking, but agreed to go along with what he said.

"Let's go now!" Que ordered.

Doing as told, we walked out of Slyy's dressing room laughing and talking. No one even noticed us leaving his room because they were too busy talking, eating, and doing interviews. Raven and I immediately fixed a plate of food, then started eating and laughing like nothing happened.

"Why does something crazy always happen on tour?" Raven whispered to me.

"I don't know, but these secrets have got to stop," I replied quietly.

We didn't talk about what just happened because we were petrified, but we saw Que giving people high fives, talking and acting normal.

A few minutes later, I saw Akira walk into Slyy's dressing room. Terrified, Raven and I looked at each other. My heart was beating so fast, I thought it was going to jump out of my chest.

Que had also seen her enter the dressing room, and he walked over to us with a smile on his face. "Take some pictures with me," he simply said.

We took several pictures together and were interviewed by a couple of reporters. We just continued to talk and smile for the camera.

It seemed like everything stood still and became quiet when Akira came running out of Slyy's dressing room. She was covered in blood, screaming and crying. No one could hear what she was saying, but you could see the blood on her hands and clothes.

The camera crews immediately stopped what they were doing and started filming her. We were right in the middle of an interview, when Akira, who was hysterical, collapsed on the floor.

All of the media started running towards her, taking pictures, filming, and asking her a thousand questions.

Slyy's security grabbed Akira and pushed her into a corner to question her, while Garrett and another security guard ran into Slyy's dressing room with the camera crew right behind them filming.

"Call an ambulance!" Someone shouted.

Knowing exactly what was going on, we didn't move. Within seconds, the backstage area was in an uproar. Janice rushed into the dressing room that was now filled with people.

Raven, Que, and I rushed into Slyy's dressing room to blend in with everyone, but we stayed close together.

"Oh, shit!" Que said quietly as we entered the room.

Janice rushed to Slyy and grabbed him, as his blood started covering her clothes and hands. I grabbed my mouth to keep from hollering. I was getting light-headed and feared I would faint.

"Control yourself!" Que whispered in my ear.

Garrett was freaking out, yelling, "What happened? Get up, Slyy!"

People were trying to calm him down, but he was going crazy. Seconds later, they were making everyone leave the room. As the building's security put handcuffs on Akira, she cried and yelled for them to stop.

She was struggling with them to tell her side of the story, but they took it as her resisting arrest and knocked her to the floor.

My heart fell to the ground. I wanted to say something, but I didn't want us to go to jail. So, I kept my mouth shut and stared in disbelief. Raven was speechless.

The backstage area was now full of police officers, and the paramedics were in Slyy's dressing room. When the police officers questioned us, we told them that we didn't know what happened, and that we only saw Akira running out of Slyy's dressing room in a panic.

"What type of person is Akira?" The officer asked us.

No one had an answer because we really didn't know her. So, we told the police that she had just started working with us and kept to herself.

The once happy backstage area was now full of hysterical individuals. No one was allowed to enter Slyy's dressing room or leave the building. His door was closed and the backstage area was now quiet.

"What's going on?" We kept asking, but they only continued to tell us to step back and move away from the door.

A few minutes later, Slyy's door opened and Garrett came out crying and saying, "They couldn't save him."

I peeked in the room and saw Janice crying and holding Slyy in her arms. I was traumatized, and it seemed like I had gone deaf temporarily.

"What did you say?" I asked Garrett.

As tears flowed down his face, he said, "Slyy's dead!"

Everyone went ballistic, and I fell to my knees. I didn't expect Slyy to die. We didn't know his injuries were life threatening.

The coroner put Slyy's body on a stretcher and covered his entire body with a white sheet. It was true; Slyy was dead.

Garrett made a tearful announcement to everyone. "Slyy was stabbed in the jugular vein in his neck and bled to death. He was already dead when the ambulance arrived."

Completely stunned, Raven, Que, and I backed away from the door. There were no words that could explain how we felt.

"What have we done?" Raven asked.

"Shut the fuck up! Don't say nothing!" Que demanded.

"Oh my God," I whispered in shock.

"Keep your damn mouth shut," Que told me.

Raven and I were extremely nervous, but Que seemed relaxed. Que was from the streets, so he was used to seeing someone die, and he didn't believe in snitches.

"I'm not going to jail for this," Que said.

"You killed him," Raven whispered to him.

"I wasn't trying to. I was just trying to help and things got out of hand," Que replied.

"I can't believe he's dead," I said quietly.

"He had been raping and beating you, Music. His ass deserved to die," Que responded with a cold-stone look on his face, showing no emotion. "Don't think about doing anything crazy. Remember, you both were in the room with me. So, if I go down for this, you're going down with me," Que said seriously.

"This is fucked up," Raven said.

"No one knows what happened. Unfortunately, Akira got caught up in this. Slyy's better dead anyone, because he can't tell anyone what happened. I knew he wasn't going to survive an injury like that. Oh well, that's the way it goes," Que stated nonchalantly.

"Damn, that's cold," I responded.

"Do you want to go to jail?" Que asked.

"No!"

"Well, you better get yourself together. Do we have an understanding?"

None of us wanted to go to jail. So, that meant we were going to keep our mouths shut and let Akira take the fall. Que gave us the rules to the game. He talked to us but didn't look at us, keeping his composure the whole time.

"Don't talk to me or anyone else about what happened," he said. "If you never mention it, you won't get caught up in anything. We're flying home tomorrow, so do everything as planned."

"Oh my God! Why is this happening?" Raven asked.

"If they ask you what happened, tell them you don't know and didn't see anything. We'll get back in contact with each other in a few days. This will give us time to see what's going on," Que continued.

"Okay," Raven and I said.

"I don't have time for this bullshit because I have to prepare for my tour. You guys are still dancing for me, right?" Que asked.

"How could you be thinking about business at a time like this?" I replied.

"The show must go on. I'm not about to let this stop me. Rehearsing for my tour will keep our minds off of things," he said.

"I guess," Raven responded.

"You don't have a job now, and I know you're going to need some money soon," Que said.

"Que, you're ruthless and don't give a damn about Slyy's death," Raven shot back.

"What's done is done. I can't change it, so I got to keep moving," Que said nonchalantly.

"Damn, Que, you're really coldblooded," I told him.

"Just go home and keep your mouth shut."

After listening to Que, I realized my childhood friend had turned into someone who was cruel and only thought about making money and succeeding. The business had tainted him, also.

CHAPTER 31

By the time we arrived home the next day, the story was on every television channel explaining that Slyy was killed by one of his dancers. It was headline news. Akira was charged with the murder and her picture was shown all over the world.

I couldn't listen to the television, radio, or read anything about the incident. Although I hated Slyy and truly felt he deserved to die, my conscious was bothering me. I didn't want to go to prison for his murder.

"Did you see the news?" Raven said as soon as I picked up my telephone.

"Yes, I saw it."

There was silence on the telephone for a short while and then we both hung up. We wanted to talk about it, but we knew Que was right about never saying anything to anybody.

Lady Mam flew to California to bail Akira out of jail. While she was waiting for her trial, she was doing interviews with everyone to plead her case. I turned on the television to hear what Akira was saying.

The reporter asked her, "What happened the night Slyy was killed?"

Akira insisted that she was innocent and said, "When I walked in the dressing room, Slyy was lying on the floor bleeding."

The reporter ripped into her, asking, "How did you get blood on your clothes and hands? Where were Slyy's security guards?"

"I had blood on my hands because I was trying to help Slyy, and his security guards were escorting Janice around backstage," Akira replied.

You could tell the reporter did not believe her and was happy they had someone to blame for his murder. I felt terrible for her and wanted to help, but I couldn't.

The media was constantly disrespecting Akira by saying she was a whore and trying to take money from Slyy. Anytime there is something dealing with sex and a woman, the woman always comes out looking bad, and it is usually other women that are pointing the finger. She was innocent and no one believed her.

My days of torture were over and no one knew my secret but Raven and Que. We now had a huge secret to keep, with theirs being much bigger than mine.

Akira continued to do interviews on every station and still claimed she was innocent when Slyy was laid to rest. Slyy's funeral was a three-ring circus. Thousands of celebrities, friends, family, co-workers, and fans came to show their respect.

Janice had arranged for everyone that was a part of Slyy's tour to be escorted to and from his funeral, and kept us away from the media. We were still all devastated by his death and tried to cope with it the best way we could.

Janice was holding up well, but we knew she was slowly breaking down. She was on a mission and said she was not going to stop until Akira rotted in jail.

We were extremely sad about his death, but everyone still had to think about what they were going to do about their jobs. Slyy was dead and there would be no more shows. One moment, our job and money were secured, and the next minute, we were unemployed.

Although we were bereaving the loss of Slyy, we had to worry about our next paycheck. Most of the band members had already lined up new tours to work on. The rest were depressed and still trying to figure what to do.

Raven and I were secure because we were going to be working with Que. I really didn't want to go on tour and needed a break, but I also would need to pay my bills soon. I didn't save my money the way I thought I would. Instead, I spent money foolishly.

Raven was just as emotional as I was, but we knew we needed to keep moving to keep from going crazy. Raven really didn't need money because Slyy had given her plenty.

Janice kept us secluded for a few days after the funeral. With the press hounding us, she checked the entire crew into a hotel, where we stayed in the penthouse suites and waited until everything died down. This made it easy for us to grieve in private.

We were feeling so guilty that Raven and I became sick. I kept vomiting and Raven constantly felt faint, but Que seemed to be holding up fine. I needed peace, and right now peace meant keeping my mouth shut.

I was scared to death and didn't know if they would actually find out that Que killed Slyy, while Raven and I stood there in the room witnessing it.

~~~~~~~

After being home for a couple of weeks, I was able to sleep and relax. Que had been bothering Raven and I about starting rehearsal for his tour, but we were in no condition to dance and were still traumatized.

We ignored his calls for weeks, but knew we would have to talk to him sooner or later. Or at least figure out what we were going to do for money.

"Why haven't you answered your telephone?" My mother asked as soon as I picked up my phone.

"I'm sorry," I responded sadly.

"I've been worried sick about you. I heard about Slyy's death on the news. Are you okay?"

"I'll be alright."

"Music, I really need to talk to you."

"Not now, Mom. I don't want to hear your I-told-you-so speech."
~~~~~~~

"That's not what I want to talk to you about. I'm on my way over."

"No, Mom! I need some time alone, and I don't feel like talking or having visitors."

"Music, listen to me! I really need to talk to you."

"Mom, please! This is difficult for me. Give me some space!" I screeched.

"Hold on. Someone is on my other line," my mom said, then clicked over.

"Hello," she said.

"Did you talk to Music yet?" My auntie asked her.

"She's on the other line now, but she doesn't want to talk to me."

"You have to talk to her."

"I'm her mother, and I still can't make this girl talk. She's so stubborn."

"You have to tell her," my auntie said, while my mother was quiet. "You have to tell her now!" My auntie demanded.

"I don't know how I'm going to tell her," my mother finally said.

"You should have been told her, because now she really needs to know that Slyy was her biological father."

"I know. I have to tell her the truth. I will talk to you later," my mother said before clicking back over to me.

"I'm back," she said sadly.

"Mom, I'm going to call you later," I told her.

"Please call me so we can talk. It's very important."

"Okay, Mom. Just give me some time and I will call you."

"I love you, Music."

"I love you, too, Mom. I'll talk to you later."

I had no plans on calling my mother back. I knew she just wanted to rub it in my face that my dance job didn't work out. I was going to avoid her until I was ready to talk, which wouldn't be anytime soon.

Right in the middle of my thoughts, Que called. This time, I answered. He immediately asked, "How you doing?"

"I'm doing much better. I just needed some time to think," I told him.

"Have you spoken to anyone about what happened?" He asked.

"No! Have you?"

"Don't be stupid," Que replied.

"This is crazy."

"I still don't know why you didn't tell me that Slyy was raping and beating you. You know you can talk to me about anything."

"He threatened me. I was scared and didn't know what to do."

"That's fucked up. You got to stop letting people run all over you. Are you sure you're okay?"

"Yeah, I'm good. This has definitely made me a stronger person."

"I know I can trust you with this secret, right?" Que asked.

"Everyone has secrets, and it seems like that's all I do is keep them."

"Tours are always full of secrets. That's the life on the road. Either you can hang or you can't," Que responded in a serious tone. "Are you ready to start rehearsing for my tour?"

"I don't think I want to go on tour anymore. Life on the road is too much for me. Too much stress, chaos and secrets. I'm thinking about taking a long break or just retiring from dancing," I said sincerely.

"I know you're not going to let these things stop you from living your dream. You've worked too hard to get to this point!" Que said.

"It's not what I thought it would be."

"But you love dancing."

"I will find something else to love."

"But it won't pay you like dancing on tour does. Your bills are going to start piling up, and you don't have any jobs lined up to pay them. You got to get over this and move on."

"I know."

"Shit happens, but you have to keep moving."

"Is it that easy?" I asked him.

"Yes, especially when you have goals and dreams you're trying to accomplish."

"It seems very easy for you."

"By any means necessary, I'm getting what's mine," he replied

"I need to make a change."

"You need to get tough and take what's yours."

"You might be right."

"You will be going on tour with me. What could be better than that? Don't stop doing what you love. Come on and get this money," Que said.

"Get the money, huh?"

"It's tons of money to be made in this business. You now know how life on the road is, and you're used to the craziness and the bizarre atmosphere. You know how to handle it, so it shouldn't bother you anymore. This is your life. Stop running from it. You know you don't want to go back to a regular job."

I looked at the bills piled high on my table that will eventually be hard for me to pay if I didn't get any dance jobs. I took a deep breath and said "When is rehearsal?"

"That's my girl! We start next month," Que happily replied.

I took another long deep breath and exhaled.

"Is Raven dancing?" He asked.

"If I'm dancing, she'll do it."

"Good. I'm trying to hook up with your girl."

"You don't know her like that."

"That's why I'm trying to get to know her. Stop hating, Music."

"I'm not trying to stop you, but Raven's not," I quickly stopped talking before I revealed her secret.

"Raven's not what?"

"Nothing."

"Just call Raven's fine ass and tell her to be ready to go on tour with me."

"Okay."

"Pack your bags because we're going to Atlanta for rehearsals so we won't have any distractions," he informed me.

"That should be fun."

"We're taking a tour bus to Atlanta since flying is too dangerous," Que added.

"Touring is a life that I've grown accustomed to, but one that I've also grown to hate."

"Music, it's not that bad. All tours are different."

"I hope your tour is much different from Slyy's tour."

"Now that you know the rules of the road, it will be a much smoother ride. Just make sure you keep your mouth shut while you have time off."

"Don't worry, I won't talk to anyone."

"Get some rest, and I'll see you and Raven next month," Que said.

"Here I go again," I mumbled to myself, as I hung up the telephone.

I know going on tour with Que is going to probably be even crazier than Slyy's tour. I don't know what to expect, but I'll prepare myself for more drama and more chaos.

Never want something so desperately, that you will allow others to mistreat you.

THE SEQUEL

TOUR SECRETS 2

BY W I N K K

MISLEADING

BY W I N K K

WWW.WINKKATME.COM